Fry Me
a Liver

Also by Delia Rosen

A BRISKET A CASKET

ONE FOOT IN THE GRAVY

A KILLER IN THE RYE

FROM HERRING TO ETERNITY

TO KILL A MATZO BALL

Fry Me
a Liver

Delia Rosen

KENSINGTON PUBLISHING CORP.
http://www.kensingtonbooks.com

KENSINGTON BOOKS are published by

Kensington Publishing Corp.
119 West 40th Street
New York, NY 10018

All Kensington Titles, Imprints, and Distributed Lines are available at special quantity discounts for bulk purchases for sales promotions, premiums, fund-raising, and educational or institutional use. Special book excerpts or customized printings can also be created to fit specific needs. For details, write or phone the office of the Kensington special sales manager: Kensington Publishing Corp., 119 West 40th Street, New York, NY 10018, attn: Special Sales Department, Phone: 1-800-221-2647.

Kensington and the K logo Reg. U.S. Pat & TM Off.

ISBN-13: 978-0-7582-8203-3
ISBN-10: 0-7582-8203-6
First Kensington Mass Market Edition: January 2015

eISBN-13: 978-0-7582-8204-0
eISBN-10: 0-7582-8204-4
First Kensington Electronic Edition: January 2015

10 9 8 7 6 5 4 3 2 1

Printed in the United States of America

Chapter 1

Before I get into how a good day went horribly—no, make that apocalyptically—bad, I'm going to tell you something you probably already know. But it's important that I put it out there since—well, thereon hangs part of the tale. It's the part of the story that isn't a mystery but is the glowing beacon of hope in a sometimes dreary world.

Before I become freakishly poetic and you think the real Gwen Katz has been body-snatched—the hard-nosed, men are really starting to annoy me, give-me-liver-or-give-me-death Gwen Katz—what I have to say is: there are several kinds of family.

First, of course, there's the family you're born with. The *tantes* and siblings, your cousins and your *bubbes* and, of course, your parents. I've talked about some of those before. The father who abandoned my mother and me; the uncle who left me his deli in Nashville; the elders who came from impoverished shtetls in the Old

World and were filled with muddy, gray-sky wisdom. Or as my father's mother used to pronounce it, "visdom." It's funny; I still hear the word that way in my head every time it's spoken. We'll get back to most of those people from time to time.

Second, there are the friends you make. The neighborhood kids, the schoolmates, the fellow athletes or Chess Club companions, the people you meet on the train or at the bus stop or at the gym, or friends of friends who become your friends and sometimes stay your friends when the original friends disappear.

Finally, there are your coworkers. These men and women are often the closest type of family, since you spend most of your waking hours with them. In my case, I'd toss in a few of our customers at Murray's Deli as well, regulars like mail carrier Nicolette Hopkins, bus driver Jackie and her auto mechanic girlfriend Leigh, banker Edgar Ward, and advertising executive Ron Plummer. In many ways, they're the closest type of family because you become involved in their lives. Not in the same sticky way as you do with family and friends who assume they can rely on you or intrude on you or—*vay iz mir*, worst of all, borrow money from you. No, these are people who affect you and move you and become part of your life because you rely on one another all day, every day, and become bound up in their problems and joys and hopes and disappointments— big, medium, and small.

The lovely part of it is they also take an interest in *you*. Some of it is sweet and superficial, like when mail carrier Nicolette suggested that we print "forever menus" with no prices or when personal banker Edgar recommended that we offer "frequent farfel" cards for fans of our pasta or dear advertising man Ron who said he thinks we should sponsor a contest offering free food for anyone who catches a gefilte fish in Percy Priest Lake. Even the negative input has value since it unites us, like when we give what-for to Luciano Doody, the personal trainer who comes in and orders tea at least three times a week, scopes out people who eat more than they should, then openly solicits them to train with him and, if they turn him down, loudly denounces their body fat ratio. Or when the staff ribs me each time Jackie and Leigh make suggestions that, while flattering, are not personally interesting—though, talk to me in a month or two or three if the drought of intelligent men continues. Which brings me to nauseating Robert Barron, the treasure hunter who lives on a boat and continues to ask me to come "rock the deck" or check out his main mast. And the newspaper publisher with questionable ethics, Robert Reid, who will do anything for a story, including pretending to be straight to date me. And more troublesome of all, Stephen Hatfield, the local slumlord, who is rotten to his nonexistent soul but charismatic as the devil. I didn't want to date him but I did want him. Fortunately, I had alert and God-fearing staff to talk me out of that.

And lest I forget, there are the delivery people we like or don't like or don't see because they come too early in the morning, or the oddities who give my staff agita which they transmit to me with knowing looks, like the witch who has teeth tattooed on the outside of her mouth, the fussy ladies of the Repeat Returner Club who only order bargain plates, and the ever-changing rainbow of music industry types, local politicos, loud cell-phone-talking students from Tennessee State University, etcetera, etcetera, etcetera. We smile politely when they arrive and sincerely when they go. We chat for a minute when we can't avoid it and pretty much everyone goes away happy. In their wake, my staff and I bond in the way that bomber crews and astronauts do when they're on a mission.

As you must have gathered by now, for me the only real family I have is the one I'm with twelve hours a day, six days a week. It isn't just that I have no real friends down here, since I haven't the time or energy to socialize; it isn't only the lack of blood relatives in New York and elsewhere around the globe; the fact is, I really *like* these people. They're my people, my crazy *shmendricks*.

For those of you who came in late or have lives and have simply forgotten The Saga of Gwen Katz, my affection for the crew came in quick stages. First, when I opted to move down here after my divorce, I only knew from accountancy and finance—not latkes and herring, except to eat them with applesauce and chopped, respectively. These people not only showed me the ropes because they had to, they did it because they love this place. There's my African American, evangelical, fifty-two-year-old manager Thomasina Jackson who never met a crisis that a loud, heartfelt "Lawsy!" couldn't stop dead in its wicked tracks. She believes so strongly that Jesus is by her side that I swear there are times I can see him. Or maybe I just want to see a young Jewish man with grace, I don't know. There's my young, tatted-up cook Newt Spengler who opens the place each morning and fancies himself a wit and a stud; I can only attest to the former and he is as witty as most twentysomethings who tweet and blog, which is to say he's more snarky and rude than clever. Born in a trailer park with forebears who hail from Louisiana, Newt was on his way to ruin when Murray hired him. The teenager had been stealing components from high-end cars when he was caught. He spent six months in prison before he was paroled and my uncle was the only one who would give him a job. Thom doesn't entirely trust him and keeps one sharp eye on the till, but in all the time I've been here there's never been a discrepancy.

On the scale of sweetness, Newt is far surpassed by young busboy Luke, who has a good, good heart even if his brain is closed to everything but his music and his girlfriend. Not that there's anything wrong with that; he's probably the happiest of us all, even though I don't understand a lot of what he says and fail to see how he's going to survive in the world if pop star lightning doesn't strike. He didn't finish high school but, God bless him, at least he works hard and doesn't seem to mind it at all.

Rounding out the team is my fortysomething waitstaff Raylene and A.J. They are the older sisters of the group, telling the kids how they should and shouldn't live with the provocative certainty of a schoolyard bully picking a fight. There's A.J.'s daughter, A.J. Two, who works here when she's home from school. And then there's my only hire, the young, pierced, dyed-buttered-popcorn-yellow Dani who has the afternoon to dinner shift and has just moved in with her boyfriend, Luke. I forgot to mention that Luke has a band, the Gutter Crickets, who play local gigs whenever they have the time and aren't squabbling among each other. I've heard them in person through two layers of wax earplugs and I've watched the YouTube videos. Their mixture of punk and folk—which they call "polk"—isn't my cup of meat, but the audiences who show up seem to enjoy them. Dani is singing with the band now, the Yoko who is causing friction but is tolerated because she knows how to get the attention of the crowd in ways that have nothing to do with her voice.

As you've probably gathered, their individual and collective moods are my moods. Their industry inspires my own efforts. We go through daily labors together, relying on one another to get several big jobs done six days a week: setting up in the morning, serving breakfast to an ocean of people in a hurry, followed immediately by brunch, lunch, and early dinner, cleaning in a way that will satisfy the fussy health department, doing inventory, storing deliveries. We go through the joys and hard, hard personal blows together. I worry about them, and they about me, when they're here, and I think about them when they're not and know what they're doing even when our place of business is dark. In the case of the deli, we've even shared a number of deaths together, from the freakishly unprecedented to the openly homicidal.

That, hardly in a nutshell, is the core of my life. There are times I feel blessed and there are times I feel stressed, but I never go to bed angry because of anything they've said or done. That makes our relationship very, very rare.

I have enjoyed that unprecedented feeling of family for the past twenty-one months. That's how long it's been since—in case I've failed to mention it, or, if I did, I like mentioning it as often as I can—I divorced my rat of a former husband, Phil Silver, and left my career as a Wall Street broker behind, moved to Nashville, and took over the deli run and founded by my late uncle Murray, whose father was a butcher and who secretly wanted to have a career as a song-writer. They were very large shoes to fill—as a restaurateur, I mean—not just among the loyal customers but among the staff.

Almost two years after my arrival, the entire staff is still here. Given the fact that my husband and father both betrayed me, that's a pretty impressive accomplishment. Though I'm sure, from their perspective, I'm the outsider who's still here . . . not them. In a way I guess they're right.

Whichever point of view is true, they are family. The one I inherited. The one I love.

The one that was about to take several hard hits in the *kishkes.*

Before I get to that, I have to tell you about other developments that have shaken up my world, including one that I sort of helped to coordinate but which fell into the "another rejection" column when it finally came to pass.

Detective Grant Daniels, my rugged, handsome, smart-enough-for-a-while and within certain noncultural parameters, one-time boyfriend—also a somewhat belligerent, controlling former boyfriend, an advocate and protector who smothered with his shielding embrace—got married. He took as his bride a WASPy member of the Metropolitan County Council of Nashville. According to the *Nashville National* website, the future husband and wife met at a budget meeting where they were on opposite sides of what to do with Homeland Security funding.

Councilwoman Suzi East—who had higher political aspirations—wanted to use it to protect Nashville's landmarks from any potential attack; Grant argued that it was more important to protect infrastructure, especially the power grid. They continued the debate over a late dinner and that was that, according to an article personally reported by publisher and big-time gossip Robert Reid.

I always suspected that Grant wanted to get into politics; insert punch line here, seeing as how he did in fact get into a politician. The cynical and possessive part of me wanted to believe the whirlwind wedding wasn't just two smartish, kind of cold human beings finding one another but Suzi looking to bolster her image among unions and law enforcement for a run at the mayoralty and Grant looking to take a political spouse for a stab at the state legislature and beyond. I also held fast to the notion that he grabbed her on the rebound from me. After all, what man wouldn't feel lonely, lost, looking for a place to put his key after being cut off from Gwen Katz?

Okay, there were a few. Most recently, Yutu White, an Eskimo I met while breaking and entering Robert Barron's boat, which is probably why he thinks I'm easy. I haven't heard a word from White since he headed back to the tundra, but then I didn't expect to.

Maybe I'm wrong and Grant is in love. Maybe I resented being proven right, my suspicion that

he was like Tarzan swinging from vine to vine.
He wanted and needed the one he was holding
on to but when that was done and he was fully
committed to the next lady, I was gone. Sure,
he stood by me while white supremacists and
Chinese gangsters had threatened my life, but
after that I didn't get so much as a coffee-to-go
courtesy visit.

Whatever the case, mazel tov and *tsai gezundt*,
say I. But here's where I get to the point—about
my work family. The Grant–Suzi knot got tied a
month before and while I felt relieved not to
have him on the periphery of my life, hovering
with longing like a puppy, I had to deal with the
sidelong glances of my staff wondering if I were
really okay—though only Thom had the chutzpah to ask. Even when I told her yes, her brain
registered it as no. Especially when I took on a
new project: renovating the somewhat dated,
1970s rural, Bonerwood Drive home which my
uncle and my father had shared for years with all
the run-downedness inherent in two straight
men cohabitating. I had a classic, bad-porn-film
fling with the new carpet layer, which was mo-
mentarily lovely. But most of my free time was
spent looking online for everything from shrubs
to bathroom fixtures to make the place truly
mine. That seemed to reinforce Thom's theory
that I was depressed. Just the opposite, I assured
her. It meant that after all this time I had finally
decided that I would stay in Nashville.

I'd been woefully back and forth on this

since I set foot in Tennessee—the home of Davy Crockett, for God's sake, not guys like Bernie Madoff, whom I understood. Fighting Wall Street bears I understood. But real ones? With just a knife?

For nearly the entire time I'd been down here I felt as if I were a foreign exchange student. As a rule, things move slower and people are more spontaneously conversational—not like the crazy people who talk *at* you in Manhattan, or ignore you while they text, but truly sociable.

So what decided me, you may ask. It wasn't the work family or the breakup with Grant Daniels or the fact that I really had nowhere else to go. Oh no. It was something I didn't see coming.

The decision took about five seconds and it came during my first visit to a shul since Uncle Murray died. I'm not religious, but I took a drive to Memphis after what I called the Chinese matter—my most recent brush with murderers—to clear my head. I passed a temple and went in. A temple is like a McDonald's: wherever you are in the world, inside they are pretty much the same. The same services, the same trappings, the same books, the same familiar Hebrew writing and text, the same rabbinical wisdom that springs from the same five millennia of culture and teaching. I realized that "home" is portable, transferable. What I missed in New York City were familiar trappings, what I grew up with; the stuff that mattered, which I should've learned from *The Wizard of Oz*, is inside. When she left,

Gwen Katz was in danger of being defined by the hustle of Wall Street, the jazz of the night life, the sanctuary of a tiny apartment crammed with personal *tchokes*. It was time I defined myself. I couldn't do that in a metropolis where every street held memories, the ghosts of thirty-plus years of previous incarnations of Gwen. I had to stop being the divorcée who was running from Phil Silver and embarrassed by her life in a corrupted profession. And now, it was also time to start over.

That's why I stayed. That's why I redid the house.

That's why I wanted to explain about work family, about how and why it matters. For now, at least, men can come and go. But not my staff. And certainly not in the way that was about to challenge us all.

The deli was very crowded today. I was expecting that and had come in earlier than usual, surprising Newt, Luke, and the other setter-uppers. Business was generally excellent and growing. Even in the winter, when the temperatures were in the forties, Nashvillians had to eat and we did a bang-up trade in both soup types: chicken and matzo ball. We also had split pea with ham for the unrepentant gentiles. Downtown was constantly alive with tourists and students, natives and transplants, familiar faces and new ones—many of whom are surprised to find a Jewish deli in this so-southern city. It didn't hurt that just awhile back we had won the Best Midrange Restaurant of the Year.

That recognition, awarded by the aforementioned Mr. Reid of the *Nashville National* and a local association of business and civic leaders, is what triggered a situation none of us could have envisioned.

Democratic Mayor Louis Benedict Dunn was an occasional customer, coming in an average of once a month with two or three aides, typically for a late working lunch. It wasn't just that he liked our mushroom and potato knishes, which he did, but it served him well to be seen at local eateries, especially one that had nabbed local kudos. It showed that he respected the judgment of the very influential communications mogul and the other local luminaries who voted for us.

But, today, this being an election year—and it being the heart of the election season—Mr. Dunn's rival, businesswoman Tootsie Pearl, was going to be at the deli *avec* media. She had come by three times in the last month, once to eat and twice to shake hands. Dunn was a green advocate and a popular civil rights attorney who had done a lot of pro bono work for minorities. Ms. Pearl, a Republican, was the founder of Tootsie's Toppers, a hat shop that became an Internet sensation after football players' wives were seen wearing their hats at a televised Tennessee Titans game. She was all for healthy living, but only when the city could afford it. Right now, hybrid car tax breaks and the banning of plastic grocery store and takeout bags were not on her to-do list as they were on Dunn's. She was about fixing the local economy and attracting jobs to Nashville.

There was also a third party candidate, Moss "Com" Post of the Edenist Party. He was an organic farmer and an unabashed Luddite who believed in a complete return to nature. He was not Facebooking, Twittering, or anything else electronic. He was campaigning on horseback and handing out bags of homegrown chives. They weren't bad. He also had a core of Republican followers, since he was a strong gun rights advocate.

A month before the election, polls showed that Dunn was expected to lose by a *sakh*, as they say in Yiddish—a lot. Unlike the blue staters, people here were less concerned about social issues than they were about the local economy, which was pretty crummy. Moreover, Post—whose family went back two hundred years—was expected to siphon off traditional Democratic votes.

This would be a good time to point out that I am not terribly political. When I was growing up, my family was always all over supporting Israel and I gave money to plant trees whenever I was guilted into it. Back then, things were simple. Just like before Clinton's impeachment, for me, things were simple: what a John Kennedy or Lyndon Johnson or Eleanor Roosevelt did behind closed doors stayed there. The press didn't talk about it. Now, there was too much information and too much parsing of every word spoken by a politician. It was all too big to get my head around. I always voted, usually for candidates who lost, and typically for Libertarians. It's not just pushy men I want out of my face; I would be happy if every wanna-be authority figure got lost. That included the government. Defend our shores, police the streets, and let us take care of everything else. That was the entirety of my political philosophy, though I'm not militant about it. Why get all worked up over something I can't control and have such a supernaturally small say in?

Anyway, Tootsie showed up at eight a.m., shortly after we opened, in order to hit the coffee-and-bagel-to-go crowd. It was a bigger deal than it had been a couple of weeks before. She was not only the favorite, she had Candy Sommerton of WSMV Channel 4 News in tow. The forty-year-old politician had grown into a genuine crowd-pleaser. Five-foot-ten, leggy, bosomy, with a big smile, big eyes, big red hair, and adorable little freckles, she was divorced from a truck driver and had once lived in a trailer park. It was a great American success story with a photogenic heroine.

Candy Sommerton was some of those things too, but she was also a major pain in my *tuchas*. I couldn't blame her for trying to get stories. Truly. The local TV market was now a national Internet market and a viral video could make a newscaster famous. But some of the stories Candy chased had to do with me and crimes in which I happened to be a victim or an innocent bystander. Candy did not understand or care to understand the word "privacy." She just showed up and expected cooperation. Intellectually, I didn't blame her. Personally, I wanted to give her a *potch* with a skillet.

One member of my waitstaff, A.J., was not only unimpressed, she was put out. Customers were in the aisles, standing precariously on chairs and taking pictures, most of them in the way of her getting her job done. Oddly, Raylene, my other morning waitperson—a term I found clumsy, however politically correct it was—was energized. Just goes to show how one person's stress is another person's fuel.

"This is all so exciting," said the southern-born gal as she waited by the heat lamps for a side of hash browns.

"Yeah, like trying to tune a guitar in the middle of a set," Luke offered. He smiled. "Hey, cool idea. A tuna guitar. A guitar shaped like a fish."

"Brilliant," A.J. said as she breezed by. "And you, I just don't get," she said to Raylene.

"Why not? This makes me feel like I'm at the center of the world!"

"Yeah, surrounded by molten lava," I said.

She looked at me quizzically. "Honey, this is big! This is American democracy at work. Don't you feel a thrill in your blood?"

"I feel it," Luke said as he stacked clean coffee

cups. "Like, I'm plugged into the Foundational Fathers."

Raylene rolled her eyes but didn't bother to correct him.

"What I feel is the overkill," I said. I nodded toward Candy. "This is media carpet bombing at work."

"You're funny," Raylene said. "This li'l pork roast is filling seats, filling the till, getting us publicity—and you're, what do you say? Kuhvetching?"

"Kvetching," I corrected.

"That's what I said," Raylene protested.

"You didn't, but that's not important. It's like Wall Street. I've always preferred slow, steady growth to a steroid injection. That's why I never really fit in up there."

"'Up there,'" Luke said. "Don't let Thom hear you. Only heaven's 'up there.'"

I happened to look over. *I heard!* Thom mouthed from the cash register.

Raylene grabbed her plate and said over her shoulder. "You're a 'fraidy cat, lady. I think I would have *killed* with all those traders and hustlers. I always liked hunting squirrel with my brothers. Never shot less than any of them. Never."

"A squirrel is a very different kind of rodent," I pointed out.

Raylene smirked as she left.

I marveled, again, that I had anything in common with this cobbled-together family of mine. Then again, it got me thinking. For me, as a young girl, the biggest challenge was getting home from school on the subway without having my *tuchas* fondled, or pretending not to notice when I was sitting across from a flasher. In the days before cell phone cameras, that was a daily occurrence. And it reached across all socioeconomic lines, from the homeless to clergy. I wondered, briefly, what my life would have been like if I had been able to carry an air rifle and plug the pervs the way Raylene shot squirrels.

Tootsie stood out front for about twenty minutes, shaking hands, signing campaign posters, and posing for pictures as people walked in. There were a lot of new faces, a lot of flashing lights that obscured some of those faces, and a lot of enthusiasm. There were a few kvetchers too, mostly about the doorway and aisle being blocked; Thom cleared a path like Moses parting the sea. Protestors were kept behind a nearby barricade by police, and there were only four or five of those. Most of them were opposed to Tootsie's support of allowing the display of the Confederate flag in public places.

Inside, Tootsie circulated among the diners. I had given my permission to do this as long as Candy and her camera operator didn't try to follow through the closely packed tables; with backpacks and purses hanging on chairs, it was tough enough for the waitstaff to get through. One slow circuit later, Tootsie made her way toward my office. I had been standing there most of the time, arms folded, watching, to make sure that things didn't get out of hand with the candidate or the TV duo.

The office was located midway along a corridor that ran from the back of the counter to the kitchen. It was situated right behind the restroom, which spoke to pretty lame design work; it was like a prewar New York apartment where every burble from the radiator or the toilet—and not necessarily your own—made its noisy way through pipes over your head. I can only imagine that when this place opened, my uncle didn't spend very much time in his cubbyhole. I not only heard water moving through the ceiling, but people humming, talking on cell phones, clearing their throats, and—well, everything else one would expect to hear coming from a lavatory.

The kitchen was active. Newt was at the grill and fryer; he seemed a little grumpier than usual, but he was young and that was to be expected. Luke had just done his midmorning restroom cleanup and was bussing. A.J. and Raylene took care of their own oatmeal and cereal orders. I usually pitched in during lunch, when I prepared the sides like cole slaw and potato salad. For breakfast, all I did was throw *shmear* on a bagel and act as shortstop when the waitstaff got backed up.

There were people out there I didn't know. There was hubbub that annoyed the regulars. I felt like I should go out and schmooze them, but

I'd only be in the way and that would make things worse. I hustled over to Thom, told her to give the regulars ten percent off. She gave me the thumbs up. She'd seen their agitation too.

Then I went back to observe. But not for long.

Chapter 2

After about twenty minutes of additional glaring, I was called to lend a hand. The morning was different in one other way. As Tootsie circulated, there was a knock at the back door. That was where we got our deliveries. The door opened onto a fenced-in asphalt area with the Dumpster and a narrow alley from the street. We typically got our bread, veggies, and fish well before opening; our butcher was behind because of two days of vegan protests at his shop, billed rather awkwardly as "Forty-Ate No Meat Hours." I was glad to see Sandy 'Fat *Fresser*' (Yiddish for a big eater.) Potts, the zaftig daughter of Alex Storm, the owner. We had a run on chopped liver that morning, which was one of our biggest sellers. It was delicious, yes—more on that later—but people responded to the Yiddish saying that Uncle Murray had put in English next to the chopped liver platter listing on the menu, as he did with most of the entrées: *Gehakteh leber iz besser vi gehakteh truris*: *Chopped liver is better than miserable troubles.* As I invariably explained to all our first-time customers, chicken soup got all the credit, but it was really the iron-rich liver that did all the heavy lifting.

The young woman was a powerfully built gal, five-foot-seven with arms like Popeye, only she looked like she lived on a diet of bacon, not spinach. She had the three big plastic-lined boxes on a dolly which she rolled in.

"How you doing?" I asked as she arrived like a blast of sunshine.

"Me? I'm personally not so bad, Gwen."

That was an odd answer. I thought for a second, then bit. "How's your daughter?" Bonnie was her eight-year-old by her live-in boyfriend, Fred, an aspiring artist. I bought one of his oil paintings, *Pickles and Cream Cheese,* for fifty bucks and hung it in the lavatory. Not because I didn't like it, I lied to his face, but where the public could see it and hopefully commission a work. That was a year ago. "Is Bonnie still a little overachiever at school?"

"Ordinarily, yeah. But my little lamb's in a kinda bad way right now."

"Why? What's wrong?"

"She's with her dad instead of doin' her numbers and letters like she likes. Poor thing busted her leg last week playing soccer in gym."

"Ow. Serious?"

"Compound fracture. Required surgery."

"*Gevalt!*"

"Yes ma'am. Fred's bringing her home from

the hospital today." She added wryly, "Lucky for us he's unemployed so he can take the time."

"Is an artist ever truly employed?" I asked.

"He is when he's a house painter. He was pretty disappointed when they put her leg in a brace instead of a cast since he wanted to paint a warren of bunnies on it."

I gave her hand a little squeeze. That was a topic for a longer talk and a few drinks. I'd only met Fred once, at a reception for Nashville Women in Business. He reminded me unfavorably of my dad, who didn't mind being "kept" by my uncle.

I had her put two of the boxes in our big walk-in refrigerator and the other on a wooden pallet next to the stainless steel worktable in the back. That kept the tub from sitting directly on the floor, something the health department frowned on. I cut one box open with a knife.

I gave Newt about three pounds of raw chicken liver for broiling, not sautéing. That was how you removed the blood to make it kosher. Then I grabbed the mayo, onions, and a jar of my special additive: diced dill pickles. Uncle Murray noted in his recipe book—which was so thick no rubber band could hold it together, it took one of those old book-straps—that the juice made all the difference. As I started to wield my Ginsu knife, A.J. came back to make a chopped liver platter from what was left in our dwindling stock. She took it from the walk-in, right inside the door on the right.

"I always thought I would like the spotlight,"

she said as she plunked it on the table and began tearing lettuce leaves from the head we kept in a stainless steel bucket of ice.

"What do you mean?"

"As a girl in a woodsman's shack, you have your 'over the rainbow' moments when you imagine being somewhere else," she said. "I thought I'd like to be on TV. We only got three channels in Kingsport, but I loved reruns of Dinah Shore." She shook her head. "She was so sweet, always smiling, always singing. But y'know—I never imagined what it'd be like having to live with lights in your face *all* the time, like this. Not just at the studio but when you went out to dinner or to get the newspaper or anything."

"Man, I'd squeeze out a live bird's guts for that," Luke said as he arrived with bins of dishes and silverware. "And the money. All that crying over being *famous!*"

"Quality of life matters too," I said.

"*Quality* is being rich and successful," he said. We ignored him.

"So the loss of privacy would not be so inviting?" I asked A.J. as I *chop-chop-chopped* the onions.

"Privacy, shmivacy," she sneered. "I'm talking about the actual spotlight, Gwen. The light itself. That lamp turns my lines into shadows like the erosion at the creek near my house. I saw myself on someone's cell phone yesterday. My crow's feet look like tiger claws."

"Dinah Shore looked okay, as I recall."

"She had makeup artists on staff, Gwen! Her skin must've looked like a tractor road in real life."

"I see," I said as I *dice-dice-diced* the pickles. "The good news is, think of how amazed people who see your photo will be when they see you in the flesh. They'll be struck speechless at how good you look."

"Good? What they'll *think* is that I got work done on my face, honey!" she said. "That would be awful. I hope I'm not steppin' on any Botox here, but I think a woman should be herself from waist to forehead and all stops in between, all those worrying, childbearing, age-wearing lines and sags. Far as I'm concerned, I earned those battle scars, and I don't want anybody thinking I had it easy."

"All fair points," I said. I wasn't one for surgery, either, though I wasn't quite at the age where I thought it might actually be necessary. I hoped I stayed true to that conviction.

"Hey, you can start wearing bikinis," Luke said as he engineered a controlled crash of a bin overflowing with coffee cups, saucers, and spoons on the stainless steel ledge adjoining the industrial-size sink behind us. Every time he did that, things clattered without ever breaking. The young man could be annoying but he was a pro.

"I'll wear them if you will," A.J. replied.

"That doesn't even make sense," he said, with a little more edge in his voice than usual.

Something was troubling him. Probably money, from the way he was harping on it.

"Fine," A.J. said. "Then you can wear Speedos."

"Boss, give me the word and consider it done," Luke said. He began washing some of the flatware by hand. We would need it before the morning rush was through.

"Luke, did you remember to replace the towel in the bathroom hand dryer?" I asked, happily changing the subject.

"Of course," he replied.

"And I say again, we need to get a hand blower. That old cloth thing is totally tragic," Newt shouted from the grill.

"Blowers don't work!" Luke shot back.

"They work," A.J. said. "You're just impatient, like most of your generation."

"That's not it! They don't dry and they leave me with cracked skin that hurts when I play my riffs."

A.J. didn't answer him. Apparently, one front during morning combat was enough.

"And I wasn't the one who brought up bikinis, Luke," she said to the busboy. The lady was never one to leave an argument unresolved, which meant her winning by force of argument or simply running out the clock. "Men are always happy to promenade with their manly assets on display. But, hey, *you* try lookin' good in some of the stuff we have to wear."

"You can look good if you work at it," Newt joined in. He stepped into our peripheral vision and flexed an arm as much for his own pleasure as to make a point. "Free weights and two hundred curls every morning."

"What do you do to build your mind?" she asked.

"Argue with people who think they know everything," he replied.

"That's enough," I said. He wasn't naturally this belligerent. Best to end it now.

Newt flexed his arm again and winked as he went back to the grill to flip some turkey bacon.

Gevalt. Though I had to admit, Newt was a hunky guy and I did briefly wonder if a Chippendale approach one night a week—one *late* night a week—would do any kind of business. I could call it *Borsht Beltless.* It could draw not just the ladies but the gay men, a demographic that didn't really have a restaurant hangout—just the usual bar or two. It was something I would have to ask our clients, not my staff.

"Look, this all started because I was just commenting about the cameras," A.J. said as she trimmed the platter with pickle slices.

"No, it started because you can't accept the fact that I would love it," Luke told her. "Lights and fame. Attention. Money."

"Rats, any idiot with a gun can get that," A.J. said. "It doesn't take any kind of talent whatsoever to get famous."

"I want the spotlight, but only for my music," Luke said solemnly. "And for Dani. She looks so hot on YouTube."

"Hey, chief—you want him to wash the coffee

cups or go to Styrofoam for the sit-downs?" Newt asked.

"Wash," I said, happy to be back on the matter at hand. "And don't call me chief."

"Yes, boss."

Except for Newt's extra little edge, this kind of banter was the norm. It made work go faster for the crew; it made me meshuga because it was an endless cycle of thrust and parry with no one ever really winning. To wit:

"Yeah, Luke, the washing might give you Newt's manly biceps and make you more of a rock star," A.J. muttered with just a soupçon of sarcasm.

"You had to start again," I muttered.

"Does a possum eat garbage?" She winked.

"You want to watch, A.J.?" Luke flirted.

"Only if I can laugh," A.J. retorted.

I shot her an exasperated look and Luke made a smug little face as he continued at the double sinks behind us. They were located right beside the basement stairs, which were beside the back door. On the other side of the door was the walk-in cooler where Sandy was just finishing up with the delivery: wrapped slabs of tongue, corned beef, and pastrami, all waiting to be seasoned à la Murray's recipe book. She put the meat beside plastic tubs of cole slaw on the bottom shelf which we had prepared the night before. The butcher's daughter swung around the refrigerator and out the back door to put the dolly back in the van. I noticed a man

in a ragged sports jacket was outside at the
Dumpster, his back to me. I wasn't surprised
to see him and I didn't mind. Unlike New York,
where the problem of the homeless seemed
overwhelming, there was something I could do
about it here. I left Styrofoam containers of food
out back. Anything that wasn't going to last another day went to feed those who needed it,
stacked in a big steel-mesh shelf that hung from
the fence. A.J. had described it as a bird feeder
for the poor, and while that had a demeaning
sound, that's pretty much what it was. As long as
there wasn't a breadline each day, I would continue to do what I could.

It would be another half hour before I could
start grating the fresh livers into a bowl. I
scooped up the last slices of what we had left, cut
it into a Tupperware container, and mixed in
some of my ingredients. A.J. plopped it on her
platter.

"I'm so glad I don't have a son," A.J. said.

"What, a college girl is easier?"

"By a mile," she said. "I've *been* where my
daughter is. I know where she's going. I know
what's in her brainpan. So, yeah. I don't know if
I could deal with Newt's kind of testosterone. It's
like those guys at the counter."

A.J. nodded in that direction. I looked under
the heat lamps at a row of intense young faces.

"Who are they?"

"The local political bloggers," A.J. said as she

used an ice cream scoop to fill a second plate with chopped liver.

"Ah. I thought I didn't recognize them," I said.

"They're all playing for alpha dog status," she said. "They're like the other bloggers who come in after morning rush, when you're in the office. They like to have stuff up by lunchtime for their readers, they tell me. They tippy-type away at the counter between sniping at each other and shooting what looks like spitballs."

"Look what I miss when I order potatoes."

"Oh yeah," A.J. said. "They actually fight on the counter for elbow room, like babies. Jab, poke, jab. Thank God we don't have those kinds of wing nuts here except for an hour or so every day."

"No, thank God I have you to deal with them," I pointed out.

A.J. gave one of her short "damn right" nods. She was the one who happened to mention that as the number of laptop and tablet users grew, we needed to establish a no-refill policy at the counter. Otherwise, people would have stayed there like it was Starbucks. Dani was the only one who didn't mind; she was happy to have fewer tips and less work. That gave her more time to hang with Luke in the kitchen. Young love. I never had it like that. The time between graduating high school and getting my MBA was a wall of study, like scholars bent over the Torah. I dated, but that was more a biological function than a social one. I emerged from the process a fully rounded grown-up. When I finally looked around at men, I settled for someone I liked well enough and figured everyone else would approve of. Looked good on a spreadsheet, like everything in my life, before it suddenly didn't.

Sandy came over with the meat receipt for me to sign. I didn't bother checking the delivery; her father always got it right.

"You got anything special planned for Bonnie's homecoming?" I asked.

"Just a hug," Sandy said. "All I've got time for."

"Let me know if there's anything I can do."

She smiled appreciatively as she looked away from the diner and down at the order form. "What're you gonna do when candidate Post wants to make the hand-shaking rounds with his horse?"

"I'll call your dad."

"My dad?"

"Tell him we've got cat food on the hoof."

"You're cold," Sandy said, but she smiled.

"I'm from New York," I reminded her. "That's not exactly horse country. Dogs and pigeons, yes—"

"Oh, shoot," Sandy said, looking up from the order form.

"What?"

"I just noticed a line item, the kosher dogs you ordered. They're in the truck."

"How could you forget that?" I laughed. "No one else buys 'em by the tub."

"That's why I forgot," she said. "They're in the

back. I came to you first instead of last, like usual."

"Because I needed the liver worst—"

My own bad joke was the last thing I heard before a big, ugly noise pounded the left side of my head.

Chapter 3

I can tell you just a little of what happened next, but only in fragments. It's like seeing everything in the shards of a broken mirror. I remember the pieces because they were merciless and vivid. The rest got lost in a fog. Even now that connective tissue is missing, except what was filled in by others. I wasn't hit on the head; I probably just blocked it all out or maybe the bigger moments just overwrote the smaller ones. Not to be glib about it, I wish I could remember this and block out other parts of my life.

The first thing I remember was how I felt. It was as though I'd stepped behind the turbine of a jet aircraft. A wall of hot wind punched me and did several things at once. It blasted the left side of my head so hard that my hair felt like it was yanked roughly toward the right; the roots were tugged so hard each one felt like a needle digging little circles into my scalp. The skin of my left cheek fluttered from chin to ear so hard

I actually felt as though it might rip away. My eardrum shrieked with pain from a powerful, simultaneous bang. And there was a Creamsicle-colored orange-white light on that side, bright enough to blind my eye for a moment. I saw that light and then I saw blackness, as if my rods and cones couldn't process any more brightness and simply shut down.

All of that started and ended in the length of a single breath, though it seemed so much longer. After that I dimly recall things hitting me, buffeting me, stabbing me, not just on one side but all over. That seemed to go on a long time but was probably also just a second or two. I do know that I was in motion the entire time because one moment the floor was under me and suddenly, amidst the pummeling and pricking, it wasn't. But I didn't drop; not exactly. I think I slid, since there was a sensation of disorientation but not a *Geronimoooo!* moment. I know I was briefly in motion and then I wasn't. In fact, I was very, very still. It wasn't exactly quiet since I could hear my breath, my heart, blood rushing through my ears, and the occasional muted scratch and crunch of things moving or settling around me. And voices. I heard muffled cries and moans.

My once proud and useful brain was no help. It was having a rapid-fire, rather pointless discussion with itself about earthquakes, plane crashes, and boiler explosions, sifting through possibilities as if it were a sweet but faulty computer in a Pixar movie. Then some godlike part of my mind took charge, shut the lesser voices up, and accepted the only thing that mattered: something bad had happened, something that made things get very dark and now suddenly unnaturally quiet, something that had apparently dumped me downward into our bomb shelter–like basement. I reasoned that based on the fact that I didn't see much light, which ruled out the kitchen, the dining room, the Dumpster area, or the street. Obviously the sun hadn't exploded or I wouldn't be thinking anything.

The first order of business, according to my super-brain, was to try to move. I realized that my body wasn't hurting but I wasn't sure it could *do* anything. I was lying facedown with my arms bent so that my palms were flat on the ground on either side of my head. I started with my fingers. They flexed and felt jagged earth beneath them. I must have fallen on top of what used to be a floor. I shifted my shoulders. My arms moved and I heard the muffled sound of rocks hitting rocks. No, concrete hitting concrete with that distinctive *chink*. I hadn't caused that but I had to make sure I didn't cause something else. I arched my back up slightly, heard more little things falling. I raised my *tuchas*, did little snow-angel movements with my legs, and rotated my feet slightly at the ankles. Next, I extended my arms like a tightrope walker, my fingers making little spidery movements. They crawled over debris of all kind, dust and stone, glass and metal, most of it small. I was intact, at least as far as my skeleton and musculature went.

Nothing was numb or hurt, so nothing was broken.

My nose tickled and I realized the air must be full of particulate matter. My nostrils were becoming more clogged with each breath. I snorted out inelegantly and breathed through my mouth. The air had a pasty quality. If I lived so long, that could cause problems one day. Who knew what kinds of materials were used to build this place?

Time for step two: the advanced audio test. I could hear dusty things dropping. What else?

"Hello!" I said in a voice that was surprisingly hoarse and soft. Whether it really was on the quiet side or whether I just couldn't hear myself, I didn't know. I also couldn't tell whether it was hollow sounding because I was in a confined space or because my ears were ringing like wind chimes. Whatever hole I and anyone else had fallen through had been covered by whatever got knocked down around it.

No one answered. I tried again.

"Hello? Anybody hear me?"

"I hear you."

The voice to my left was raw, choked, but definitely Thomasina. It sounded close, but then with ears that felt crammed with matzo brei everything sounded near—like the way you hear things underwater.

"Thom, are you all right?"

"I—I—maybe . . ."

Her voice trailed off. That didn't sound encouraging. Thom was a big woman and despite standing most of the day, she didn't have the strongest heart in Tennessee. She put her trust in God, not in lower cholesterol, to make things right.

"Stay calm and stay put," I told her.

There was another voice, this one to the right.

"I hear you too," said Luke. His voice was stronger than Thom's. It sounded like he was closer, maybe two or three yards away.

"You okay?"

"Seem to be," Luke said.

"I'm here too, Gwen." That was Sandy. Her voice was coming from somewhere below my feet. Her throaty exclamation was accompanied by a tumble of rubble. Whether it came from her moving body or of its own accord from above, I couldn't be sure. "Listen—your manager is partly under me. She's breathing but I think she just went unconscious."

"Restin'," Thom said faintly.

As I suspected, Thom was not okay. "All right, everyone, stay put. I'm going to try to get up," I said.

"Do it slowly," Luke said. "I've got things all around me—don't want to dislodge anything."

"Fine, stay put."

I sniffed. I didn't smell the gas that fed the oven, which was good news. Sandy was a smoker. She might have matches on her, in case we needed them.

I struggled to push myself from the ground. Until I did that I didn't realize how much debris was on my back, but it was small pieces. It slid thickly off to the sides like seawater from a breaching whale. I made it to my knees, *ouching* when they came to rest on sharp objects and adjusting accordingly. I pulled out the cloth napkin I kept in my apron to wipe spills. I shook it out and tied it around the lower part of my face; the air was full of dust, possibly from my rising, and I didn't want to inhale it. I did a 360, turning carefully on my aching knees, my arms extended to make sure there was nothing on any side of me.

"Anybody know what happened?" Luke asked.

"I was looking at my truck," Sandy hacked. "Something in that vicinity got bright and loud."

There was an ominous creaking sound from somewhere beyond and above Thom. I knew the layout of my deli better than I knew my teeth, and I flossed twice every day. That was where the walk-in refrigerator was, the area where Sandy said she saw a flash. As my ears began to clear slightly, I heard something else in that direction: voices. They were faint, like a TV in a hotel room down the hall.

"You got any enemies, Sandy?" I asked as I felt above my head, like I was doing the wave.

"Only pigs, cows, and chickens," she said.

"Better than moose and squirrel," I remarked, not sure anyone would get my Rocky and Bullwinkle reference or would be in a frame of mind to laugh even if they did. I was just trying to amuse myself; it was either that or be really, really terrified.

There was nothing above my head and, with my hands still above me, I started to get to my feet. That was when my fingers touched exposed iron. I stopped. It was slanted down, toward where Thom was lying. I touched it gingerly, felt around it. Powdery *shmutz* came flying off and I turned my eyes away. Not that I could see anything in the pitch dark; I just didn't want to get anything in them. I resumed my search and felt something that made me very, very unhappy. It was rubber. With treads.

A vehicle was sitting above us. That answered the question about what had plugged the rabbit hole into which we'd tumbled. Strangely calm, I moved my fingers along the tire toward one side until I reached a bent exhaust pipe. Simultaneously, I listened for some kind of dripping sound, trying to determine whether the gas tank had been punctured. I didn't hear anything, didn't smell anything, was hopeful that it wasn't quietly running down the chassis. It occurred to me then to step back, out from under it. I did so by feeling behind me with my feet. Inside my head, I heard Thom's voice saying, "Lawsy." I wondered if she'd somehow sent the thought, that there were other people. I was going to have to circle around quickly and make certain that everyone else was out from under it, including anyone who might be unconscious. As I began walking sideways, feeling my way with the side of my right foot, I heard another sound I wasn't happy to hear: a groaning from the direction I knew the walk-in refrigerator to be. I took some comfort in the distant voices, not just because it meant that there were people up there but because whatever happened had apparently been localized in and around the kitchen.

I reached Thom first. Or rather, my foot did. I knocked into what felt like the top of her head. I heard heavy breathing and said her name.

"I'm here," she told me in gasps.

"Okay—just relax as best you can."

She wheezed in response.

I felt above her. There was a fender. "Thom, is there anything on top of you?"

"The kitchen table, I think," she replied.

"I'm going to try and move you before God gets around to throwing the kitchen sink," I said.

"Don't—don't blaspheme," she said with a wince in her voice.

"Sorry."

"Gwen? Is that you?"

I stopped moving. "Candy?"

"Yes."

"Are you all right?"

"I don't know."

"Do you have your phone?" I asked.

"No," she said. "I was coming back to ask you about something."

"You left your phone somewhere?" I said. Whenever I saw her, on the air or off, that thing was glued to her palm.

"I did," she said defensively.

And then I understood. "You left it recording, hoping to catch Ms. Pearl saying something damaging."

She was silent. That was uncommon so I was obviously correct.

Ah, Candy, I thought. Even without the tricks, and entirely by chance, the newshound finally had her big right-place, right-time story.

"Are you in any pain, danger?" I asked.

"I'm pinned, but I seem to be intact."

"All right—sit tight."

"I had my phone but it seems to have fallen from my pocket," Sandy said. "I'm trying to find it. Tough to do that by feel."

I didn't bother to ask Luke for his phone. By mandate from the boss, he kept it in his jacket on the coatrack. I did that so he wouldn't be tempted to text Dani while he worked.

Suddenly, a white light winked on behind me. I took in the scene displayed in harshly shadowed illumination before turning. I saw Thom covered with white dust, the table sprawled top-down across her waist. I didn't see any blood but she was breathing very, very heavily. Her head was under the fender. I saw Sandy with her feet about four feet beneath the passenger's side wheel of her delivery van, which is what the vehicle sitting above us was. It was lying at an angle, the higher side being the one I'd touched first. Luke was safely off to the side. I looked back to where the cell phone light originated. I couldn't see who was behind it.

"Who's there?" I asked.

The speaker turned the light on himself. It showed a lean, smooth face with high cheekbones and deep-set eyes capped by a spray of curly brown hair. He looked to be about thirty.

"Name's Benjamin," he said. "I'm here on

vacation. I was in the restroom, just drying my hands on your quaint pull-towel and about to head out. I heard a bang and fell backward when the floor did."

"Are you okay?"

"Seem to be. Toes and fingers work."

"What about the phone? Does *it* work?"

"I tried to call out—nada. Hey, I've got someone here—a woman who isn't my girlfriend."

He shined the light to his right. The cold white beam fell on A.J. She was lying on her back, covered in raw vegetables, her eyes closed but her chest moving. "I heard her moaning a second ago," the man said.

I made my way to him, stepping over the wreck of what used to be a pegboard full of utensils. They were now scattered on broken pieces of floor tile and concrete. As I rounded Sandy's suspended delivery truck, I saw Luke ahead. He was sitting just beyond the point where the front half of the van disappeared up through the floor, like Ezekiel's battle chariot headed for the middle of the air. Actually, it looked nothing like that; I was thinking biblical because, I guess, I was kind of hoping God was paying attention.

"Luke, can you scoot over to your right?" I asked.

"Sure—why?"

I asked Benjamin to shine the phone past me. The cone of light illuminated the van like an oncoming truck.

"Holy crap!" Luke said when he saw it.

"Oh my," Sandy added. It was surprise tinged with guilt, even though this wasn't her fault.

Luke started to crab-walk away from the van, toward A.J., on his dragging *tuchas*. It occurred to me that it was a necessary but somewhat futile move; if the damn thing fell in, it would take the rest of the ceiling with it, in which case it might not matter where we were. There were other appliances above us, like the oven and fryer with its still-hot oil and the walk-in refrigerator . . . not to mention knives, sacks of potatoes and other heavy food items, people, and the structural beams themselves. If the collapse were big enough—and I couldn't tell from here—there were also the tables and chairs in the dining area, the counter, the cash register, and my office.

"Should we be moving everyone toward the walls?" Sandy asked. She was looking around in the light, the same as I was. "It seems to me the ceiling would hold up better along the sides, like standing in a doorway during an earthquake."

"Unless the walls fall over," I pointed out as I made my way toward A.J.

"Oh, Jesus," Sandy said with sudden understanding.

"I hear people up there," Luke said.

"I know. Probably getting them out of the deli." This supposition was supported by the fact that while my hearing was getting clearer, the voices were getting dimmer.

"I assume you're Ms. Murray?" Benjamin said.

"I'm Gwen Katz," I told him as I knelt between

Luke and A.J. "Murray was my uncle. You're from Philly?"

"I was an undergrad there. How did you know?"

It may have seemed like an inane question given the circumstances, but I was trying to keep my mind *off* our circumstances.

"You pronounced 'Murray' as 'Merry.'"

"I see. Haven't lived there in a while, but accents die hard."

"Welcome to Nashville," I said.

I removed the napkin and cleaned the powder from A.J.'s face. I touched her neck. The pulse seemed strong enough. I took her cheeks gently between my fingers, moved her head from side to side. She didn't moan. I slid my fingers under her head, felt a damp spot. I lifted her head from the concrete shard it had struck. Luke pulled it away and I lay her head back down, on the napkin.

Suddenly, another light flashed on, a big one coming from behind me, from the direction from which Candy Sommerton's voice had come. It was different from the other light, less pure, more yellow: a big, industrial flashlight. I looked over at a strangely inverted face.

Candy Sommerton was lying not far from her new camera operator, Washington Waverly, who was about three feet away to the right. They were both on their backs, their legs raised slightly higher and bent at the knees, resting on rubble. They looked like astronauts in one of the old Gemini space capsules, wide-eyed and alert. The camera was half buried by debris, the lens crushed. I took all that in before the cameraman turned the flashlight back toward me. I imagined it came from the utility belt he was wearing.

Benjamin shut his phone to conserve the battery while, under the glow of the flashlight, I picked through the icebergs of rubble on my way to the newshounds. The bottoms of their legs, from about the knee downward, were lost in a stack of Sheetrock and wood that was stacked at least five feet high. I could see nothing in the darkness beyond, but I knew what was there: a roughly six foot high room with an oil burner, the water heater, and the water mains that ran toward and then under the street.

"Well, pickle me pink," I said as I started over.

"That's a little flip under the circumstances, don't you think?" the newscaster asked.

"Under tense circumstances, that's what I do," I replied. "I get flip. You should see my divorce transcripts." I reached the duo and took the flashlight. I ran it up and down the wall of debris. "I think you'd better stay there—I'm afraid of what might happen if I tried to move anything."

"Human Jenga," Waverly said.

I smiled. "Welcome to the Borsht Belt South."

He smiled up at me weakly. Candy was busy rotating her jaw, pushing an index finger around and about behind her ears, apparently trying to pop them.

"If you two are finished smart alecking, what the hell're we going to do?" Candy asked.

I shined the flashlight up and down, then back and forth across the wall of debris. It looked like a stage set from here, complete with ominous props, a cast in jeopardy, dramatic lighting.

"The first thing we're going to do is get everyone to the other side of this mound," I decided.

"Why?" Candy asked.

"Because the floor above is the dining area and the street—probably a lot more sound than what's directly on top of us. Benjamin? Luke?"

"Yes?" they answered in unison.

"There's a spot to the right—see it?" I shined my light toward the right, where the wall that was piled on Candy and her cameraman dipped lower and lower, like some Roman ruin. It was only about three feet high at its lowest point. "Let's get everyone over there. Once they're on the other side, I'm going to try and get these two out."

"Try?" Candy cried.

"If this stuff on top of you falls forward, you'll be a lot worse off—"

"Than if that van drops and comes forward?" Candy asked.

She had a point. I had thought about it dropping but not continuing in the direction it was facing, running her over. The vehicle was not moving but it was creaking—along with the section of our ceiling that was supporting it. But those might be internal sounds, like the engine and steering wheel column, that sort of thing.

I looked back. In the faint light, I could see Luke and Benjamin gently raising A.J. as a prelude to carrying her over. To my right, Sandy was starting slowly, painfully, to get to her feet. She reminded me of a quarterback who had been sacked hard on knees that were already wobbly. Sandy could help me with Thom and then we could turn our attention to these two.

"All right," I agreed. "Just sit tight while I see to Thom."

"Like we have a choice?" she said.

"See? I knew you had some funny in you," I said. "I'm going to move Thomasina and then I'll get something to climb on so I can push the pile toward the oil burner on the other side, away from you."

"Be careful where you push," Waverly said.

"Sure, but why?"

He looked backward at me, over his forehead. "Because I think my camera landed there."

"I'm sure it's insured—"

"Not what I mean," he said. "I was turning to shoot the diners when everything went nuts."

"I still don't—"

"He may have caught the explosion," Candy said.

Chapter 4

Things had been so messy and disorienting I hadn't given any real thought to the cause of the blast itself. That would come, of course, but not right now.

I knew this basement like I knew my own handwriting, which was to say very, very well. But in the near-dark, it was unfamiliar. All the color had been replaced by three shades of gray: moldy gray, cadaverous gray, and granite gray. Visually, there was no hint of health or life. Motion? Yes. Life? No. The outside sounds I was accustomed to hearing down here were gone or thickly muted, rendering them unfamiliar. The sounds down here were heightened. Every move was accompanied by a shifting of sharp-edged stone or debris—a cold, serrated sound. I could hear my breath and, when I was near other people, their breath too. And speaking of breath, the air was musty, dusty, and dry. It filled my nostrils with a cottony film. The temperature, usually open-oven hot in the summer, skating rink cool in the winter, was a strange mix: chilly with waves of body heat slowly taking over. Whether we knew it or not, we were all perspiring, all afraid. Debris from the kitchen jutted from the ground like a lunar landscape; a bent colander, a shattered carving board, the silvery slicer. I said before that it was like a stage set. I was accustomed to seeing those with a script. With a cast in fake jeopardy. With the ending known to someone. This was still only the first scene in the first act.

I had never been in a disaster, except on the outside of an event like that of the World Trade Center, and my brain and body just did what it had to from moment to moment. There was no past, no future, only "now" with multiple and pressing demands. I couldn't afford to dwell on the things I did not know, like who did this and why, though a corner of my mind could not help working on the puzzle of the blast.

I had assumed the explosion was something in the kitchen, most likely gas—the combustible kind, not the *greptsy* from eating *grivenes* kind. But I wondered if that were the case. I hadn't smelled anything, and then there was the timing. A mayoralty candidate was in the deli. Was she the target? If so, who would want to kill a mayoralty candidate for Nashville in a deli? Or anywhere else, for that matter?

I watched as the young men carried A.J. over. Her arms hung limp, swaying at her side, her fingertips scraping the debris field. They had found a plank to put her on, hoping to minimize as much as possible the impact on any broken bones or internal injuries she may have suffered. I worried about internal bleeding. Holding the flashlight, I placed her arms on her chest as we worked her up and over the breach in the wall. Then we went over to where Sandy was helping to free Thomasina. Sandy was mostly feeling her way in the dark shadows outside that pale cone of the flashlight. I could hear my manager's strained breathing, hoped she was not keeping something serious from me like a heart attack. She was like that, worried about others first. It wasn't a martyr complex but a true generosity of spirit. I left Benjamin sitting with A.J., cradling her, and took Luke to lend a hand with Thomasina. With some effort, the three of us got my zaftig manager on her bloodied legs. She winced as she draped her arms over my shoulder and Luke's, her fingers clutching our backs with sharp, painful fingernails. I let her hang on; she needed it. Sandy held the flashlight and hobbled after us as we went.

"I'm sorry to be such trouble," Thom said.

"Don't make me hit you," I replied.

She snorted a little laugh. "Lord Jesus, forgive one of us for our sins or both of us if You have the inclination. And bless Luke who suffers in silence."

He rotated his chin. "That's because your shoulder beef is in my mouth."

"She doesn't really have shoulder 'beef,'" said the butcher's daughter. "That would be a cow, steer, or bull."

"Maybe, but 'shoulder meat' sounds kinda raunchy," Luke said.

"I'll settle for my angel wing," Thom said.

We all laughed as we got Thom to the wall, helped-her over—she winced but did not cry out—and then I left Sandy with my apron and told her to clean and bind her injuries as best as possible. Benjamin was using his cell phone to explore the little cavern with its rusted iron pipes and dragon of an oil burner. Then he turned to Washington's camera. He *fumfitted* around there for a few moments.

"This baby looks fried," he said.

Washington craned around. "You talkin' about my camera?"

"Yes, and I mean that literally. There's a coating of solid white grease, still warm. Looks like it got inside."

"Damn. *Damn.*"

Benjamin stood at a crouch, continued to shine the light around. "Is there a way back there?" he asked.

"Not for us," I told him, "though I imagine that's how rescuers will try to get in. The far end, where that big rusty pipe runs transverse into the bigger, rustier pipe, is under a sheet of dirt that's beneath the sidewalk. It'll probably be a helluva lot more solid than the rest of the floor."

"Maybe we should bang on the pipes, let them know we're here," Luke suggested.

"Okay, but let's throw things at the oil burner."

"Why?" Benjamin asked.

"They'll get a floor plan, know exactly where that is."

"Good point," Benjamin said.

He looked around, grabbed stone-size pieces of debris, and hurled them. They hit with a series of dull bangs. A few more flakes descended, like something shaken off by a slumbering giant. If anyone heard, they made no sign.

"There's probably a lot of commotion up there," I said. "The sounds might be lost in that."

"Yeah, and I'm not too crazy about this banging stuff," Sandy said. "You ever seen those avalanche movies where someone shouts and brings down a cliff?"

"I have," Luke said. "I've also seen movies where people are trapped with a killer."

He was probably being glib, but I had to admit he had a point. I was pretty sure of Sandy, and I didn't think Candy would go that far for a story. But we knew nothing about Benjamin. Or the target, if there was a target.

Benjamin was crouched, froglike, tenderly holding A.J.'s right hand in his. Maybe he was a naturally sensitive guy. Given my current suspicion about the goodness of all men, of any man, I stayed out of that mental debate. All that mattered was whether or not it helped A.J. feel better. That decided, I settled in with the others. We had gathered in a kind of Lord of the Flies circle around the glowing cell phone in Benjamin's other hand.

Washington sighed a big, disgusted sigh. He

was a linebacker-big hillbilly with a wispy beard and whipped prune accent to go with the look. He was on his knees like he was waiting to be baptized.

"So what do we do, just sit here and trim our fingernails?" the camera operator asked.

"Given the flakiness quality of the ceiling, I think that's the best thing," I said. "The sitting and waiting, I mean."

"Why?" Washington asked.

"For one thing, Sandy is right," I said. "Fumbling around or even loud noises may cause something to fall. We don't know what's propping up what. For another, and perhaps more importantly, if we make noise we may not be able to hear any instructions that are called from above."

"Good point," Luke said.

"Like we could hear anyone now?" Washington asked. "I like being proactive, man."

"I agree," Candy said. "You think sitting in one place, under a ceiling that could be ready to fall on our heads, is a *good* idea?"

"Maybe not good, but better," I suggested.

"Uh-uh," Washington said. "Gettin' *out* is a better idea. In case you didn't notice, there ain't a lot of good air down here and it ain't gettin' any fresher."

"So stop talking," Benjamin said.

Washington's small eyes seemed to double in size.

"Benjamin is right," I said. "And moving around will only use it up."

"I see. And who made you lead coon dog?" he asked.

"My place, I'm in charge."

"What is this, martial law?" Candy asked.

"Nothing so sensible as that," I said. "Who're you gonna sue when this is all over?"

"What?" she asked.

"According to my insurance policy, the safety of customers and suppliers on my premises is my legal responsibility. I want to be able to say we acted cautiously and rationally."

"Waiting to be suffocated or crushed ain't rational!" Washington said.

"I'm with him," Candy said. "Jesus, Gwen. I can't believe you're worried about money at a time like this."

My spine went cold. "Money?"

"That's what insurance is," Candy said.

"I hope you're not saying what I think you're saying," I said. I hadn't really faced a lot of Jewish stereotyping since coming to Nashville, but this was the South and my radar was clearly set to "sensitive."

"I'm saying that your priorities are messed up," Candy said.

"That, from a woman whose job it is to push her way into tragic situations and bust them up with a can opener."

"Ladies, civility," Sandy cautioned.

Candy had leaned forward. Now she settled back. That was her nod to civility. "My job is about reading people," she said. "In case you haven't noticed, it looks to me like my camera operator is having a panic attack."

I looked over. Washington seemed embarrassed by the revelation. Candy gave him a sympathetic look. So did I. Candy might have been an empty talking head on TV, but she was right about Washington and she was also right that I hadn't noticed. I saw a faint sheen forming on his leathery skin and it wasn't from the stuffiness. His eyes were moving about, his head making restless little birdlike movements forward and back.

"It's not panic—it's the air," he said. "I just need to breathe."

"Washington, can I make a suggestion?" I asked.

"No, you can stop telling me what to do!"

"A suggestion isn't 'telling'—"

"I said shut up!" Washington stood defiantly and gave his head a mighty *zetz* on a pipe. We actually heard it *clong* like in a cartoon. He yelped and dropped back to his knees, his two big paws rubbing his crown. Candy just looked at him sadly, like a ghostly pale Esmeralda at Quasimodo.

"My cameraman is always superfocused on what's in *front* of him, not above," she said charitably.

"Ow," he said belatedly.

Luke and Benjamin actually laughed at that. So did Washington. It was a nice relief, but the gloom settled again quickly. Washington sat and brooded, breathing slowly to try and calm himself. We all sat still now, listening. Now that we were quiet and in a smaller area than before, with less echo, we could hear muted voices from above.

"Can anyone make anything out?" Benjamin asked.

"No," Luke said. "It's like trying to hear stuff when the water's running. Thank God the boss yells all the time."

I held up my hand to hush everyone. "I recognize Detective Bean's voice," I said. The policewoman had a very deep, distinctive tone, even when it was muffled. I felt better knowing that she was on-site.

"Sounds like she's giving orders," Luke said.

"That's a good thing," I remarked. "She knows what she's doing."

Silence settled on the group again, except for the heightened breathing of Washington.

"I got trapped in a cave when I was a kid," Benjamin said. "It was up in Santa Barbara, the painted caves. I found Chumash art that had been hidden for centuries. There was a rock fall. I had to light a fire or they'd never have seen me. Talk about bad air. The cave had an opening, a chimney, that sucked all the smoke toward me."

My eyes drifted toward the tourist, who was a metallic white head floating in the glow of the phone. I wanted to get our minds off the situation; quiet conversation seemed like a good idea.

"Is that where you're from?" I asked. "Santa Barbara?"

"Originally, yes. Now I live farther south in

California—a town called Temecula, about ninety minutes inland from San Diego."

"I've heard of it," Candy said, getting into the spirit of things. "Near Murrieta Hot Springs."

"That's right."

"What do you do there?" I asked.

"I run a restaurant with Grace—my girlfriend."

"So you're a competitor!"

"Not really. We do Tex-Asian fusion."

"Let me guess," Luke said. "Your place is called TAF. No, wait. TAFFY. Tex-Asian Fusion For You."

"Actually, it's called GAB—Grace and Benjamin."

"Not even in the ballpark," Luke grumbled.

"You weren't even in the parking lot," I said. "So what's the menu like, Benjamin?"

"BBQ rib sushi, nacho pad Thai, hot and sour taco soup—that sort of thing," he said. "We came up with the idea when we were both students at the Tustin Institute of Culinary Invention."

"Sounds interesting."

"It is, and after two years we were finally doing well enough to take our first vacation."

"And you came here," Candy said, her newswoman's ears moving like a cat's.

"That's right. We love food and music so here we are."

"I'm still waiting to take a vacation," I said.

"You should come and visit us," Benjamin said.

"We keep telling her to go somewhere,

anywhere," Luke said. "We even offered to take up a collection. Thom ran things before she got down here."

Thom didn't respond and that brought things down a little. She was unconscious, breathing softly. A.J. was also unconscious but breathing a little more energetically. I couldn't tell if it was the thin air or whatever injuries they had sustained. I was more anxious about them both than I let on.

"Are those Austrian Crescents you use in the pancakes?" Benjamin asked.

I was impressed. He knew his taters. As I recall, Benjamin ordered matzo ball soup and extra crispy latkes, the lady had our homemade gefilte fish and matzo brei. I didn't ask what he thought about the meal; I knew those were aces so it wouldn't really matter.

"It's a mix of those and Yukon Gold," I replied. "They're kind of the classic for latke-making, but I add my own little twist."

"A secret?" he asked.

"Very."

Candy had put her arm around Washington. She shook her head. "I don't understand how you can talk about potatoes when we're buried in your basement."

"You know what?" Washington said. "They should keep going. I'm hungry. It's taking my mind off stuff."

"Are you serious?" Candy asked. "I thought you were really going through something!"

"I didn't eat this morning," he said. "That could be why I hit my head, why I'm so skittery."

"I sat here defending a person who was just *hungry*?" she railed.

"Say, I think a tub of chopped liver fell in with us," Luke said.

"Yeah, I smelled it," I said.

"You want some, camera guy?" Luke asked solicitously. He jerked a thumb behind him. "It's out there."

"I'll give it to you at cost," I joked. Candy didn't hear my jest. She was too busy being embarrassed because Washington was rallying.

"You got rye bread down here?" Washington asked.

"If the bread shelves fell, yeah," Luke said.

"You're all *crazy!*" Candy screamed. Perhaps coincidentally, chips fell from the ceiling. She dropped her shoulders and lowered her voice. "How can you think of food?"

"You're just frustrated because we can't broadcast from here," Washington said.

"Yes, Waverly. That *has* got me a little on edge," she admitted through her teeth. "We may have experienced Nashville's first terrorist attack and I'm sitting on both the story *and* my ass!"

"Language," Thom cautioned weakly.

I looked over at Thom and smiled. Her eyes were still shut but there was a faint look of disapproval around the mouth. If anything could rouse her from a stupor, it was godlessness.

Candy did not apologize. She just huffed and

grabbed her ankles and rocked back and forth on the jacket she had folded under her posterior.

Luke was peering into the area with the hanging van. "It's possible," he said. "And I'm thinking that some chopped liver might be a good thing to have."

"Forget it," I said. "You're not going back in there."

"The tub wasn't near Sandy's vehicle," he said.

"Dammit, Luke, we're safer here. I know you always need something to do—but this is the time to just sit."

"Again, says who?" Washington said. "For all we know, there may be a way out in that direction, behind the van."

"A van that's hanging by God knows what!" I said. "Maybe the perps don't want to risk disturbing it. Besides, if there were a way out, there would be a draft. There would be smells from the food in the kitchen. There would be *light*."

"And God spoke," Candy said.

I ignored her.

"There could just be some light junk lying across it," Washington said. "Something we could push aside."

"If that were the case, people up there would have come in through the back door, pushed it aside, and lowered a ladder by now."

"I think the fire department would have thought of that," a weak voice agreed.

Our eyes all shot toward A.J. It was good to hear her voice, however weak.

"Hey, how are you, waitstaff person?" I asked, crawling over.

"Achy-breaky," she replied. "My head feels like it took the back end of a swing for the bleachers."

"There's no blood," Benjamin said. "I checked."

"Who is holding my hand?" A.J. asked.

"I'm Benjamin," he said. "A tourist in your city."

"Thank you, tourist Benjamin," she replied, looking up at him. "Did I hear correctly or did I imagine that you are from Southern California?"

"You heard correctly."

"I have family in San Bernardino."

"Same county, not too far," he said.

"I love it out there. All the mountains and the desert—"

I sat on my knees beside her. "Why don't you lie quietly?"

"Honey boss, that's what I've *been* doing," she replied. "Like floating on a rubber raft in a pool, kinda daydreaming. I don't want to pass out again. Anybody got any water?"

I looked at the others, their heads shaking. I hadn't seen any water bottles by the van, didn't see one in here. We do not sell them so I wasn't surprised.

"Sorry, no," I said.

"That's okay," A.J. said. "I'd probably choke it up."

"Why?"

"Throat . . . clogged—," she said, then drifted back into unconsciousness.

I lay a hand on her throat. It felt cold. I had no idea what that meant. The silence returned as we all listened to the sounds from above. They seemed to be coming from the area where Washington had hit his head. It may have been my imagination but they seemed to be a little louder.

Luke looked at me. "Do you think—?"

"That they heard Washington's bang?" I asked. "It's possible." I got to my feet and tried to calculate where this pipe was. I believed it fed the small sink behind the lunch counter. That was a hollow metal basin; it could have amplified the sound like a bell. Though the deli would have been evacuated and I couldn't imagine anyone was inside, even the fire department, it was possible someone heard it. I took off one of my comfortable Tofino slip-ons, turned the heel toward the pipe, and knocked out a series of three taps. I waited and then did three more. There was silence from above and then my series of raps was returned.

"They heard!" I said.

"Woohoo!" Candy cheered. She was suddenly a new, renewed woman.

I rapped three times again, then slipped my shoe on and sat; I was standing on something wet and hoped a pipe wasn't leaking somewhere. I didn't want to have to move A.J. or Thom again if water came flooding in.

"So I expect they'll be coming in through

the deli," Benjamin said, cocking his head to that side.

I nodded as his cell phone light started to fade.

"Hey, you should probably turn that off and save the battery," I suggested.

"Whoa, wait!" Candy cried excitedly. "Benjamin, turn that over here!"

"What?"

"Put on the damn camera! I don't know why I didn't think of this sooner."

"You're going to shoot video?" I asked.

"No," Candy said. "He is."

Benjamin hesitated.

"I'll *pay* you!" Candy said. "Please! Something like this can go national, or at least viral! Just ten, fifteen seconds. I'm begging you!"

"I never heard her beg," Washington said. He was looking up, casting around hopefully for a sign of light and life.

The thought of what Candy had asked was abhorrent on one level, using our limited resources to propel her career. But I understood it. I looked at Benjamin who was looking at me.

"Your call," I said.

"Literally," Candy added. "I'll need you to send what I record down here as soon as we get out."

The young man nodded. He raised the cell phone as Candy made herself look as disheveled as possible. She moved toward the rubble wall with the sloping van as a backdrop. I had to give her this: the gal could think in a crisis.

"Ready?" she asked.

"Go," he said.

And then, as the video rolled—and on cue—the van took his direction and fell into the basement.

Chapter 5

I happened to be looking in that direction, not watching Candy but shielding my eyes from the direct beam of the cell phone flashlight. That was how and why I saw everything that happened.

It was as if the van had a ghost driver. The back end, the one facing down, lurched toward us slightly as though someone had shifted gears. It hesitated a moment and then sped down backward at a forty-five degree angle. The rear tires struck the basement floor like the landing gear of a 747 touching down, then the front end of the van dropped hard. Propelled by the fall, the entire vehicle rolled toward the rubble wall. The van was trailing two heavy steel cables that ate into the ceiling above. They were tied to the front axle; it looked as if the FD had been trying to secure the van through the back door of the deli when the floor gave way just enough to drop the vehicle through. The van traversed only three or four yards, but that was just enough for it to ram the wall. The van stopped hard and the wall gave without a struggle. The rubble toppled onto A.J.

She didn't make a sound but Candy did. The newswoman shrieked and threw herself to the side as more debris toppled toward her. Washington reached over and pulled her toward him, across debris that had fallen earlier, to get her out of the way of the van.

There was a long, thick moment of silence. Our eyes all drifted upward. The fall of the vehicle left an opening in the ceiling. The hole and the air around it were filled with a thick gray tester of particulate matter with dim, hazy work lights beyond.

The ceiling seemed to have lost everything it was going to lose. It was time to take chances now if we were going to help A.J.

"Luke, stay wide of the opening but yell at whoever's up there. Tell them we have injured people."

He acknowledged this as I spun to where A.J. lay buried. I began throwing smaller blocks toward the hole, away from the others. Sandy— who had jumped back and missed the collapse by inches—was already pulling at the rubble with her strong butcher's hands. Benjamin kept the cell phone on us even as the light started to wink out.

"A.J., talk to me," I said, more to myself than to her.

"Do what your boss says," Sandy added. "Say something. Anything!"

My fingers became claws and my heart became a locomotive. They worked together, ripping at stone with a ferocity and strength I didn't imagine I possessed. The pile on top of A.J. was nearly a foot deep. Her arms were jutting from the base, the fingers twitching. Candy crept over and pulled stones from her feet. I saw her look over at Benjamin's phone. If the camera was still running, she was probably making sure her face was on it, playing the hero. I didn't have time to be angry. That would come. So would beating the crap out of whoever was responsible for this. And I *would* find out who that was.

By the time we had cleared the mound from A.J.'s chest and face, the only light was from the craterous hole the van had made. My poor gal's head was turned toward the opening, her eyes shut. She was scratched with vivid red gashes but the rest of her was so pale, so cold, so lifeless—

I heard Luke talking softly from somewhere to my left. I didn't have the time or patience for "soft." If he was talking to himself, he needed to shut up. If he was passing information to us, he needed to speak up.

"Luke, we need help down here!" I screamed. "*Now!*"

I heard Luke say something as he stepped back from the opening. It was drowned out by the sound my heart was making as it rammed against my chest.

Suddenly, on the left, I saw figures were dropping through the opening. I saw them peripherally, as silhouettes blocking the light. They were solid shadows that I knew from the silhouettes were firefighters. They hurried toward me and I slid to the side, on my knees, heedless of my own pain. There were two figures, then three, and they continued to clear rubble away until a rigid, plastic patient mover was lowered on nylon ropes and brought over. One of the figures placed something over A.J.'s head and neck to stabilize her while another hooked something to her arm. Plasma, probably. They also put something over her mouth, then carried her to the opening and hauled her up, steadying the board on all sides with caring, up-reaching arms. I was literally sick when it hit me that it might not matter. A.J.'s skin had looked more mineral than flesh. Except for the twitching in her fingers, nothing had moved. I couldn't process the thought of losing her.

We had just been talking about little things upstairs. But though they were trivial, they were the things of life, the stuff a day and relationships are made of. How could this be? How could it have *happened*?

I wavered like a reed in a strong wind; I didn't realize I was about to fall until Sandy caught me.

"We better get you out of here," Sandy said.

"No—Thom first. I'm okay."

"Your knees and fingers are bleeding."

"Thom may be bleeding too," I insisted.

Sandy held up her hands in surrender. As the bottom of A.J.'s stretcher disappeared through the opening, the figures came toward us. Flashlights played through the dim cellar.

Floating grit was everywhere. We shied like vampires before the sunlight. I heard muffled voices, realized the new arrivals were wearing protective masks. I felt like I was in one of those post-apocalyptic movies where the military finds people infected with some government-created virus that somehow got loose.

Wait! I thought urgently. *Maybe it had, injected in calves, stored in their livers for dissemination.*

Clearly, my head was not working properly. I saw Sandy guide the next wave of rescuers to Thom, saw others coming forward, felt hands on my arm. There were foggy voices in my ear and big, blank, dark faces in my eyes, and then the world started to do cartwheels and I went down on my back. I was semiconscious as the firefighters got to me. One of them raised her mask.

"Do you know your name?" she asked.

"Moe Howard," I replied.

"Ma'am, you are not—"

"One of the Three Stooges, I know," I said. I was annoyed that I had fallen and when I get annoyed I get comically sarcastic. I started to get up, felt a stabbing in both eyes, shut them and stayed put.

"How is A.J.?" I asked. "The woman you removed?"

"I do not have that information," she said.

Why do first responders never use contractions? I wondered. Do they think it sounds more official? More believable? It failed with me because how could she not know? They all had to be plugged into the same communications units. I just didn't feel like arguing.

I was carried out on another plastic board, raised to the light as if I were ascending to heaven, then transferred to a gurney that was rolled to the street in front of the deli. I pushed the paramedics away as they tried to strap me down.

"I'm all right," I insisted, and swung my legs over the side. Hands reached for me but my shoulders wriggled defiantly—stupidly, too, since my head was still mushy. When my feet touched asphalt, I made them stay there, rigid, like I was a modern-day golem.

A medical technician came around and looked me in my defiant little *punim.* "Ma'am, we need to check—"

"I wasn't injured," I said firmly.

"You were. There's blood all over your hands and legs," the technician said, and began to cut holes in my pants.

I let her as I looked around. "Where's my friend? The blond woman?"

She didn't answer. I winced as she put some kind of ointment on my knees. My roving eyes settled on a gurney sitting beside an ambulance. I saw a hint of platinum-colored hair poking out from the top of a clutch of medics.

A.J.'s hair.

The medics were working fast, chirping instructions and information back and forth. Behind them, at a distance, I saw Luke standing and staring, Dani sobbing under his arm. He must have just been brought from the pit; Dani must have seen a newsflash or someone must have tweeted and she biked over to the deli. Raylene and Newt were behind them, hugging each other. I didn't see Benjamin but I assumed he was with his girlfriend. Or maybe Candy was with him, making sure he sent the video to her station. I looked back just in time to see Thomasina being raised into an ambulance.

That was all the motivation I needed to get myself in motion. The medic had finished patching my knees and hands and was dutifully taking my blood pressure. I tore at the Velcro armband and, ignoring her shouts, stumbled toward my staff on uncertain legs and hot, angry knees. Raylene saw me and started to cry. She extended her hands toward me, her fingers wriggling like hungry little birds, and threw her arms around my neck. I let her take some of my weight and grabbed her shoulders and the others joined in. It was a strong, much needed group hug.

"Our girls are going to be all right," I whispered hopefully. "They have to be."

"Life doesn't run on wishes," said Raylene, the pragmatist.

"No, but trust me on this: negativity makes things worse."

Raylene considered that, then nodded. "I'm going to the hospital to be with Thom. Then I have to get home—of all the days for my mother to be coming to town."

"You do what you can."

"I'm going to call A.J. Two," Newt said. "Is that okay?"

"Sure," I told him. "Absolutely."

Newt still seemed a little "off," understandably. Having something to do would be good for him.

We held the hug until I heard a familiar voice call to me. I turned and saw Detective Bean. Beyond her I saw the distinctive white truck, with a horizontal blue band fringed with gold, belonging to the Metro Police Bomb Squad. The young African American woman had spotted me and was walking over briskly. The staff dispersed as the detective put a hand on my right arm.

"I'm glad you're all right," she said.

"Physically, yeah," I said. "I can even hear now."

"I'm sorry about your waitperson. Does she have a family, someone you'd like me to call?"

"Why, is there news?" I asked anxiously.

"No, no, I just thought."

"We've got that covered, thanks," I said.

That had scared me and I felt a little weak. Bean grasped my arms, steadied me. I was okay, but by the time I breathed again, tears were running down from the sides of my eyes. It wasn't until my skin felt fresh and clean where the tears ran that I realized I was probably covered with grit.

"Why don't you sit?" Bean asked.

"Because then I *will* lose it," I said.

"I understand."

"All those things down there . . . ," I said absently.

"What things?"

"The utensils that had been so useful just moments before . . . trash."

"Some of it may be salvageable," Bean said. "It will all be recovered for us to examine, then you can go through it—"

"Twisted. Broken." That was all I could think about. That horrid otherworldly terrain with a coating of choking dust.

"Detective Daniels called to ask how you were," Bean told me. "He wanted to know if you needed anything."

"A new deli," I said. That was harsh and I added more politely, "That was nice of him."

I didn't want to think of Grant now. He was always strong when I needed him to be and strong when I didn't need him to be. I didn't want him on my mind or even peripherally back in my life. "What do we know?" I asked.

"Not much. We can save the official interview until later, but can you give me a once-over from your end?"

I told her I knew as little as she did since the blast knocked me silly and made my sensory perceptions meaningless. Bean nodded with what seemed to be understanding.

"Do you think Tootsie Pearl was the target?" I asked. "Is she okay?"

"Shaken but uninjured." Bean cocked her head toward a clutch of squad cars up the street. "We're talking to her now."

I looked over. I saw the police talking to witnesses and keeping two layers of people back: journalists and gawkers taking cell phone videos, and people who were just trying to get through or go to their jobs. To her credit or damnation, I wasn't sure which, Candy Sommerton was among the former, inscrutable and ghoulish, chasing the story. She was trying to talk to the police while other reporters were trying to talk to her, looking at their cell phones—at her video, I suspected. To add to the confusion, reporters were trying to interview the bloodied, limping reporter while she was trying to get to the mayoral candidate. The press refers to such events as a "media circus." A circus has a ringleader and some sense of order. From where I stood, it looked like the monkey house at the Bronx Zoo.

"There were no death threats against the candidate that I'm aware of," Bean confided to me. Her answer to the question confused me at first. I had forgotten what I'd asked. "We're checking the social media sites now but—I'm told you have a kind of eagle eye on your place. True?"

"I guess so," I said. "When I look out at the diner, it's like a rabbi on the High Holy Days, gratefully spotting worshipers who came every Sabbath, not just once a year, but aware of the rest."

She smiled. "So, Rabbi Katz. Did anyone look out of place?"

"Everyone was eating, if that's what you mean," I said. "I got the Homeland Security circular about profiling that was called something else. No one stood out."

I had, in fact, dutifully read the document Homeland Security sent every six months. It was a PDF brochure called *If You See Something, Say Something* and it was sent to all public service institutions. The document said in big red letters that it was wrong to profile people because of their race, religion, nationality, dress, or accent. But, that said, it advised us of behavior to look out for such as patrons being overly protective of property that did not appear to have any obvious value; seeming agitated without any direct cause, such as someone talking loudly nearby; wearing heavy clothing that seemed inappropriate to temperate weather—all the things that anyone with a healthy strain of paranoia should spot without help from the federal government.

"Who was the person down there with you?" She checked her iPad notes. "Benjamin West?"

"A restaurateur from Southern California. Said he was sampling local cuisine with his girlfriend."

"Anything suspicious about him?"

"Only his taste in food, Tex-Asian fusion."

She noted that in her file and added to that a photo she had taken of the couple sitting off to the side. Bean was probably just a few years younger than her predecessor, but there was a big generational gap in the way they handled technology. Grant was still a notepad-and-pen kinda guy.

"Any other thoughts?" Bean asked. "Random impressions—anything while it's still fresh?"

I thought for a moment, replayed the experience. "Candy said something about her cell phone being in the diner."

"We found her phone and checked for video," Bean said. "Nada."

"Benjamin took cell phone video downstairs—"

"He told us," Bean said. "We saw it. Some sensational images but nothing that helps us."

"All this technology and an explosion in a major American metropolis can still go uncovered?"

"That's the big dirty secret about surveillance," Bean said. "Not about this situation necessarily, but anyone who is smart and does due diligence can find ways not to be photographed committing a crime." She paused thoughtfully. "I think that's it for now."

"What do you think happened?" I asked. "Any impressions?"

"Not yet, and I can't really talk about an ongoing investigation," Bean said. She added, "You may not know this, but your former boyfriend was disciplined for talking out of turn about cases."

"You mean discussing them with me?"

Bean nodded.

I felt a little bad for Grant; he probably did that more to involve me in his work, to help the relationship, than to solicit my opinions, however helpful they sometimes were. When I worked on Wall Street, I always thought rules and regulations were probably a good idea. Now, I wasn't so sure.

Detective Bean folded away her iPad. "If you

want anything, water, coffee, a sandwich, there's a catering truck—"

"Detective, I have my own—"

I stopped myself. I looked away from the trucks and the crowd, back in the direction of the deli. *No*, I told myself. *I didn't.* I didn't have my own coffee machine making premium coffee ordered from my special supplier in New York City. I had a dust-filled diner that was dark and colorless, just like the basement had been. Only it seemed darker because it was so bright and sun-colored outside.

My brain was at war with itself again. Part of it wanted to grab my remaining staff, have them salvage what they could, and set up a card table on the street to get back in business. Busyness was the best thing to stave off depression and I worried that I was about to get very depressed. But the other part of my mind told me not to do that, not to subject Luke, Newt, Dani, and Raylene to that. They would probably go along with it because I asked, because it was what I needed. It was not what they needed. They needed to tend to their own, to settle their individual souls.

"Do you have a bottle of water?" I asked Bean.

"Sure," she said.

She walked to a squad car and took a plastic bottle from a compartment inside the door. When she returned, I cracked the cap and poured the contents over my head, washing my face with the other hand. Bean couldn't see the tears I let flow again but they were there, mingled with the warm water. I did not blame myself for what happened to A.J. or Thomasina. No one could have foreseen it. But for as long as I had been down here, things just went wrong at the deli. I didn't think the universe was trying to tell me something. God had to have better things to do. Still, there had been way too much pain.

He managed to make time for Job, and there *was a really good man,* I thought.

But Satan had been involved in that *mishugas.* I don't think that was the case here, just terrible, terrible fortune. *Shlimazel,* as my grandmother used to call it, but on a grand scale—like a pogrom.

Gwen, you're rambling, that small rational part of my brain said to the rest. *You have to focus.*

On what? I asked myself.

Time to call a truce. Bean went off to talk to her officers and I walked toward the deli, drawn to it like Sleeping Beauty to the spindle. I reached the police tape at the curb, went under, saw Bean from the corner of my eye motion a patrol officer who was moving toward me to back away. I went to the open door where a cloud of dust hung like a theater scrim. I stood there, staring past the cash register to the hallway with my office and into the kitchen. Except for the dust, everything seemed okay there. Beyond, out back near the Dumpster, I saw first responders and firefighters working with portable winches and video monitors. I didn't know if they were lowering people in or trying to get the van out. It didn't matter just then. What was important was that everything this side of the kitchen was fine. The fryer, oven, refrigerator, and freezer seemed intact. There was no power—we'd lose all our perishables—but those could be replaced quickly.

"Don't think about it now," someone said beside me.

I turned. It was Benjamin and his girlfriend. I returned his crooked little smile with a crookeder one, then looked at her. She was about five-three, a very slender blonde whose svelteness was a walking advertisement for Tex-Asian fusion. She had pale blue eyes, long lashes, and a big California girl smile framed by full lips. And there was a slender strand of pearls around her swan-long throat. Despite everything else that was going on, standing next to the girl made me feel ancient, unfit, undesirable, and so ethnic that I felt sure I could pass for a lifelong ortho-dox Lubavitcher.

Benjamin's hair was wet and his face was washed back to the ears. His blue button-down shirt looked blue around the shoulders, pale charcoal below. He'd apparently taken the same Evian shower I had.

"How do you know what I'm thinking?" I asked.

"Because we'd be thinking the same thing," the young woman said. She offered her hand. "I'm Grace."

I shook it. "Gwen Katz."

"I'm pleased to meet you and very glad you're

okay. I love your homemade gefilte fish," she
said. "Very delicate, not too fishy."

"Thanks." I smiled. It seemed an odd time for
a compliment but I accepted it gratefully. Any
port in a . . . "And thanks for using the present
tense."

It took them both a moment to get my meaning.
Grace nodded with understanding; the gefilte
would plate again.

I was looking at the young woman closely.
"Are you sure we haven't met?"

"Quite sure," she said. "Never been here."

"You look familiar," I said.

"With all the faces you see, I'm sure you saw
one of my doppelgängers," she said. "We all have
them—people who look just like us."

I wasn't in the mood for crazy. I turned to
Benjamin. "So you're okay?"

"That's what the medics say," he answered.
"And I feel fine."

Grace clutched her boyfriend's arm with both
hands. "It's a miracle, right? What a thing to
have happen!"

"What a thing," I repeated. That was a strange,
understated way to describe an explosion in a
metropolitan restaurant.

"Did Candy get her video?" I asked Benjamin.

"It's already on the website," he said.

"Of course it is."

"I'm happy for her," Grace said. "I'm happy
for any woman who works hard and makes it."

I didn't rebut that. I would have been happy
too if she hadn't built her career on exploitation.

Of course, my disapproval sounded tinny even to my own ears when I thought of how many women I knew who had built their careers on bad financial programs on Wall Street. And Grant's honey, Suzi East, probably had made more than a few backroom deals to move her political career forward.

What kind of payoffs or crow-eating or insurance expediencies would I have to accept to get through this *kappora*?

"One of the officers told me you've been here before," Benjamin said.

"On the outside looking in, you mean?"

He nodded.

"Yeah. Someone was shot by a sniper right through my window. I opened for takeout the next day."

"That's horrible!" Grace exclaimed. "Not that you opened, I mean—that something like that happened!"

"It was kind of a gang thing," I said. "We did bang-up business as I knew we would—"

"Because rubberneckers love their morning joe?" Benjamin asked.

"I guess there was some of that, sure," I admitted. "The stronger sense I got, though, was that people like to support their community in times of trouble."

"They like it or feel good about it?" Benjamin asked.

Oh, I thought. *Out in the daylight, he was one of those. A cynic.*

"I can only talk about the results," I told him. "It

made me feel like we were part of a community. That's all that matters to me."

"Of course," Benjamin said quickly. "I think I gave you the wrong impression. I applaud the people for their support and I applaud you. We both do. In fact, we were just talking—is there any way we can help? After all, we do know the restaurant business and I make to-die-for Hashimoto browns."

"Which are?"

"Hash browns with a wasabi butter coating."

"Maybe we could use horseradish instead," Grace suggested.

"Not bad," Benjamin said.

"Look, both of you—I appreciate it, but a new menu item is the last thing on my mind right now."

"Of course, of course," he said. "It's just a poorly timed suggestion, especially after all you've been through—"

"You went through it too, honey," Grace reminded him with an edgy little smile before turning back to me. "We just wanted to help. That's all."

"I understand," I told them. Grace's apology was actually a little belligerent. Something told me that these two weren't exactly what they said they were, though I didn't intend to waste my limited brain power on them.

"Hey," Benjamin said suddenly. "We're staying in town, at a bed and breakfast on Blair Boulevard."

"The Owlet?"

"That's the one."

"Famous for its organic pancakes and home-made syrup," Grace said.

"I know the owner, Elsie Smith," I said, once again looking at the young woman. There was *something* about her.

"Elsie's a lifelong Nashvillian, she told us," Benjamin said.

"Polite but very reserved," Grace added.

"Any interest in joining us for breakfast?" Benjamin asked.

"I don't know," I said. I couldn't think about eating or planning or even moving from this spot.

"Forgive me, Gwen, but the worst thing you can do right now is withdraw," Benjamin told me.

"I appreciate the concern and it isn't that," I said. "I'm just not sure what I'll be doing a minute from now, let alone tomorrow."

He smiled sweetly and slipped me a card. "Understood. Please call if you feel up to it, or if you need anything."

I didn't look at the card. People were always handing me business cards in the diner, mostly exterminators and food service providers. I just tucked it where I tucked everything, in my *tuchas* pocket.

The young couple departed; the police didn't need anything more from them, as far as I could tell. They were odd ducks but I didn't give them any more thought. I went back to where my staff was texting, probably letting family and friends know they were okay. A.J.'s ambulance was gone,

Thomasina had been taken away, so it was just us, we few, we who should be happy to be alive.

I *was* grateful, though as the terrible reality of what had happened settled in, I found myself doing what I usually did in stressful situations. I was getting riled up and eager to *do* something.

And, as always, I didn't have to do much. Something new soon tapped *me* on the shoulder.

Chapter 6

My staff went to the Baptist Hospital where both A.J. and Thomasina were taken. I did not go; they needed time alone. And, frankly, so did I.

I'm not sure my manager's prayers had anything to do with the selection of that hospital, or the fact that Thomasina was a passionate Baptist. But it was a fitting destination that, I was later informed, received a "Hallelujah, Lord!" when she arrived. I envied Thom the faith which events like these could not dislodge. I didn't understand it; I was, as I'd just demonstrated, more comfortable thinking things through and waiting for help than praying to God to free me. Though I have to admit, I wondered about the value of doing both. Because there went Thom, to the hospital of her choice, while I stood outside my dusty diner unable to serve customers, with nothing to do and with two employees injured, one of them seriously.

Who is the shmuck? I asked myself.

And who, I also asked myself, was the masochist. I watched from just within the police tape. Sometimes I looked inside—more was visible in the kitchen area as the sun passed overhead and came through the back door—and sometimes I looked over at Detective Bean. She talked to Sandy briefly. She spoke with people who had been in the dining area. I wondered if they would ever return. Sandy's father, Alex the butcher, arrived shortly after the ambulances left. He was in a van that was the twin of the one destroyed in whatever it was that had happened. Even before he stepped out, I heard Detective Bean ask if he wouldn't mind staying since she wanted to talk to him. He nodded.

Alex was right out of Sholem Aleichem, a.k.a. Solomon Rabinovich, a.k.a. the author of the Tevye the Milkman stories, which became *Fiddler on the Roof*, among other tales of Jewish life in the *shtetls*—the poor villages of eighteenth century eastern Europe. He was stocky, about five-nine, with monster arms, an unkempt salt-and-pepper beard, big, wild eyes, and a full white apron he hadn't bothered to remove. There were smears of blood on it. In any other circumstance, a police detective would have taken him into custody for something.

Alex Storm wasn't even Jewish. He was from New Orleans. But my uncle had called him an honorary Jew since Alex had shared his family recipe for chopped liver—though he called it Creole p'lâté . . . the *l* standing for liver. Alex did that with all the viscera pastes he made. That included p'tâté for tongue, p'bâté for brain. I liked it. Quirky charm always got to me.

As soon as Bean finished, the butcher jumped out, embraced his daughter, then looked around to find me. He hurried over, big arms in ungainly motion like a charging orangutan on the Discovery Channel. That, too, was seriously endearing.

I ducked back under the tape to greet him, my arms stiff at my sides to protect me from his big bear hug. Standing several steps back, Sandy winked at me. She knew exactly what I was doing.

"Dear Lawd, how are you, hunny bunny?" he asked with more than a hint of the Deep South in his voice.

"Relatively undamaged," I told him. His endearments were always beautifully sincere.

"Thank God, thank God. Sandy all right, you all right—I feel blessed. I'm sorry I wasn't here sooner." He broke the hug. "Forgive me?"

"Of course! Is everything all right?"

"Oh sure, sure. I was in the meat locker, ignoring the vegan activist group, and didn't hear my phone," he said. He hugged me again. This time I wasn't prepared. "I'm so glad you're all right!"

"I was."

"What?"

"I think you're breaking some ribs," I said.

He laughed self-consciously and released me. "You're sweating," I said, looking him over.

He waved dismissively. "The protestors already had me agitated and I drove like a muleteer to get here."

"Run any of them down?"

"Huh? No. I just put a curse on them using feathers, candle wax, and spit." He looked back at Sandy who was texting someone. "I swear, Gwen, I was never so worried in my life. I couldn't reach Sandy till I was in the neighborhood. We didn't have hills in Louisiana. Sandy cleared it with the law to let me in."

"I think that's because the law wants to talk to you," I said.

"Yes, so the law informed me," he said.

I was looking past him at Detective Bean. She and her iPad were approaching from the alley beside the deli. Her expression was grim.

"She doesn't look happy," I said. "That's not a good sign."

"Why?" Sandy asked, coming closer.

"Because she likes me a lot."

The detective motioned with her head. Alex pointed to himself with a questioning look and she used her index fingers to jab toward all of us. We met her at the front of a police car. The sun was warm and bounced sharply from the trunk. Alex squinted in the glare and perspired even more.

"Anything wrong?" Bean asked him.

"My friend's restaurant blew up!" he said.

"Is that why you're perspiring?"

"What? Oh, no—I'm just hot," he replied.

That must have passed muster, because Bean didn't take an iPad photo. Though she also seemed to have something else on her mind.

"The bomb squad just informed me that the

explosion was not an accident," the detective said. "Preliminary analysis suggests that a sizeable improvised explosive device went off inside a white container that, as best as we can ascertain from a badly charred section, was labeled 'plate.'"

I felt a chill. "That's p'lâté," I informed her.

"Spell it," she said, and raised her iPad.

I did, adding, "It's chopped liver, one of our biggest sellers. We had removed two out of three tubs from the truck."

"And placed them where?"

"There was one on the table to fill orders and one was in the walk-in cooler."

"Where was the third?" Bean asked.

"The third was still in the van," Sandy said. "It was a different blend, with curry, headed for one of our other clients."

"It was so labeled?"

"Curry, yes, but not with the address. I knew where to take it."

"Do you have any idea which one exploded?" I asked.

"The one in the refrigerator," she said. "The van is intact, so that rules out the curry. And you're not dead, which eliminates the other."

Duh. Bean gave me a crooked smile that let me know it was okay; it *had* been a rough morning. The detective took me by the arm and ushered me aside, motioning for Alex to give us privacy.

"Is something wrong?" I asked.

"I don't want the rest of this information

being tossed around, even by well-meaning folks," she said. "I only got to see the cooler from the doorway, but it is a pretty sturdy-looking unit. Do you happen to know the specs?"

"It's all stainless steel—I don't know what gauge or anything like that. But it was, I don't know, about two, three inches thick? And the floor has an added covering of a nonslip rubber compound. The thing is, it may have been open."

"Why? Wouldn't that defeat the purpose—"

"During the meal rushes, we're always going in and out so we don't always close the door tight. It may have been open a crack."

"I see," Bean said. "That actually makes sense, because it looks like the unit was turned slightly by the blast so that the right front edge was thrust downward like a wedge, cracking the floor by the back door, causing that side of the kitchen to slope inward, and that's what made the van roll up against the back door. The van picked up just enough momentum to go through the rift created by the walk-in. Most of the damage was caused by the weight of the van, not the explosion."

"So whoever did this may not have expected this level of destruction," I said.

"Perhaps, or they know how you work and had a good idea exactly what would happen," Bean replied.

"You really think they could have anticipated the van?"

"Anticipated? No. But perhaps someone

was watching with a detonator and seized the moment."

Great. Then there was a possibility we were being targeted. All those feelings of being an outsider, the ones I'd tamped down, came whirling back.

"What about access, Gwen?" Bean asked.

"To what? The kitchen?"

She nodded.

"Someone's in the kitchen at all times, more or less. Bathroom break is the only exception."

"Anybody outside that you noticed?"

"There was a homeless man picking up one of the containers of food I leave out there," I told her. Before she could ask, I said, "I didn't see his face. I don't know his name. He was wearing an old red blazer, blue jeans, and he had long gray hair worn loose under a black baseball cap."

"Had you seen him before?"

"I don't know. It's possible. These folks change clothes when they find something new, less torn."

"Do you ever talk to them?"

"If they talk to me first."

"Ever exchange harsh words with any of them?"

"There's no reason," I said. "They only come to me for food. I've probably spoken kinder to them than I do to most of the men I know."

She studied me for a moment. "You seem to pay pretty close attention to the people around your place."

"Closer than to the men I date," I said.

"This'll go faster without the levity," Bean pointed out.

I nodded. Mentioning Grant brought out the worst in me. "I'm a New Yorker," I said. "We have personal proximity alerts that work better than a fighter jet."

Bean laughed at that. I didn't even realize I was being amusing. My head was still trying to figure out exactly what was happening.

The detective asked for a list of everyone else I could remember seeing there that morning: full names, staff included. I provided them all. This wasn't the House Un-American Activities Committee. I did not mind naming names since I believed that everyone I knew was innocent.

And if they aren't, they deserve to be in prison.

I thought back through the morning from the moment I unlocked the door. I saw the faces in my head. I also saw my beloved little deli, intact and whole. You'd think I would be used to us being knocked on our collective *tuchases* by now—dead diners, dead catering customers, dead street musicians, dead deliverymen. I wasn't. It's like New York City. Big as it is, old as it is, that doesn't stop it from flinching. Every trauma, whether it's an attack on the city or a person, a storm, a financial collapse, each one hits a new nerve, leaves a new wound that takes time to heal. As much as traumas seem the same, they are not. The people around us are not. The dynamics are different every time.

As my grandmother used to say, *Ain sheitel holts*

macht nit varem dem oiven. A single log doesn't warm the fireplace. And a single experience, no matter how brightly it burns for that moment, doesn't provide lasting illumination.

I was pretty thorough—all those years of remembering numbers had paid off. Bean used the car to radio my information or descriptions to whomever one radioed information and descriptions to. After dating a detective for twice as long as I should have, you'd think I would have learned something about police procedures. I hadn't. Another indication that I was with the wrong guy: I hadn't been listening.

I wasn't ready to go so I continued to hang around in the protective bosom of the police cordon after Alex and Sandy had left in his van. They had waved good-bye while I was talking to Bean. I watched the forensics team scour the diner. Not that there was much to watch; they were as still as archaeologists fussing over an ancient tomb. Bean was gone. I knew from past experience that we did not have very many security cameras on the street, but I was sure she had gone off to check whatever was there.

The afternoon settled into late afternoon, with the changing sunlight, a little chill, and more and more traffic being allowed down the street. I went up to the deli window and looked inside. I also watched the reflection of pedestrians across the street and the single line of cars moving behind me. Now that I was alone, it was time and calm for me to wonder: who and why?

I truly did not think—did not *want* to think— this was a war against me, so the logical conclusion was that someone was after Tootsie Pearl *or* was trying to give Tootsie some airtime. Would someone risk killing people to make their candidate mayor of Nashville? I did not know, but it was certainly possible. I couldn't come up with a possibility B.

That was a bust, I thought.

I stood there because I wasn't sure what to do next. I didn't want to go home because I'd be doing the same thinking only with a real sense of being alone. And what would I do there, play with the cats and watch TV? Clean? This place was my life.

"I have seen it before."

I turned to the bass cello voice on my left. Oh, joy. It was Big Jefferson D. Harkins, a college hoop sensation, a black kid who broke his wrist rollerblading and never got his foul shot back. The Memphis-born onetime rising star was now a field agent for the Department of Codes and Building Safety. I had met him months earlier, when a sniper took out my window. He wore a tailored black suit, sunglasses, and a loud tie with a picture of his namesake, Jefferson Davis. He carried a digital camera in one hand and a tablet in the other. I thought of all those crappy little offices in New York that made the parts for clipboards, the wooden backs, the metal clasps, the springs, and wondered what would become of them.

"What have you seen?" I asked. I wasn't really interested in the self-impressed *shmendrick*. But like the game he used to play, local government was all about areas of responsibility. He controlled his like a little czar and, unfortunately, I needed his okay to do anything with my business. So I made nice.

He looked down at me from six-foot-seven and smiled. "Contrary to what the philosophers tell us, lightning does strike twice."

"I think it was old wives who said that, not philosophers and scientists. Because I can tell you from personal experience, the Empire State Building gets hit dozens of times a year, same spot."

"Well,"—he laughed one of those deep, condescending laughs—"a lot of you northern folk do things that are contrary to the laws of nature."

I didn't want to get into this with him. Harkins went to Thom's church. It might embarrass her if we had a row. At the very least, she'd be forced to defend me when she needed to concentrate on getting better. Yet, despite that, despite my better angels, I heard the tiny little demons in my mouth saying, "Such as?"

"Hey, I'm not supposed to expand on personal views during working hours," he said.

"Were you just in a garden?" I asked.

"On one of the greenway trails," he said. "Honeysuckle?"

"Fertilizer," I replied.

"I was checking out a storage shed," he admitted. "Anyway, there are more important things than how I smell, such as—how are you?"

"Drying."

"Say again?"

"I took a street shower with a bottle of water, courtesy of Metro PD," I said. "Other than that, I got cut up a little down there, nothing serious."

"Glad to hear it," he said. "I heard Thomasina was down there with you. I called the hospital, they told me she's serious but stable."

"That was nice of you, to check."

"The church sends out e-mails so that we can pray for our fellow parishioners," he said. "I wanted them to know her status. She's good people."

"She's very good people."

There was a short silence and then Harkins said, "I've just been inside the kitchen, Ms. Katz. I am very concerned about the structure."

That was spoken like a man who was accustomed to giving people two answers in the same neutral voice: "*You're good to go*" and "*I am very concerned about the structure.*" That latter means you're *shtupped.*

"How concerned?" I asked.

"The van appears to have compromised the floor supports."

"They're iron."

"They're bent iron," he said. "They cannot be bent back without a loss of integrity. They will most likely have to be replaced. There are also significant cracks along the baseboard in the kitchen on the northern and eastern walls. That suggests the walls have also been dislocated, which would impact the ceiling as well."

That was the analysis of someone who probably took a two year course in structural engineering, possibly when he was in college but more likely on the dime of the DCBS after he went to work there. Not that his assessments weren't valid. But I didn't understand why the city didn't just send out a qualified engineer to render a real decision instead of a middleman to give me an interim one.

"The final decisions will be rendered by our engineers and of course your insurance carrier will endorse or rebut those findings, but I do not believe they will find it advisable to reconstruct the building."

Which I owned and did not rent. Which meant the headache would be mine, all mine.

Even though I was only half listening to a semieducated dissertation that used big words to make a jock sound more knowledgeable than he was; even though I sort of knew that the building took a hard, hard hit, hearing the words "reconstruct the building" was a kick in the *kishkes*.

"What about my stuff?" I asked numbly. "In the office."

"That can be brought out by qualified retrieval personnel or with proper supervision," Harkins told me.

What the hell did "qualified retrieval personnel" mean? Half man, half Irish setter? I asked what he meant. He said I could engage an engineering firm that worked in "high risk" recovery or, if my insurance company had no objections, I might be able to go in myself along a carefully demarcated "safe route."

Blah and blah.

Listening to him was like listening to a rabbi at a funeral. The body was in the ground, I'd had my moment, and there was nothing to be gained by standing here. I didn't want to go home and I didn't want to go to the hospital. My staff had enough on their souls. They didn't need to hear this.

"Thanks," I said.

"If you need financial aid during this transition—"

"I'll be okay, thank you."

"Hey, I know you're independent and all that, but small business funds are there to be used."

"I don't believe in taking what I don't need," I told him. "Not from anyone but most especially I don't want handouts from the government." I looked up at him. "And what is 'independent and *all that*'?"

He shrugged his broad shoulders. "You're from New York City. You're a feminist accustomed to having a support group for any opinion you care to have."

"You say that like they're bad things."

"When they hold you back, they can be."

"Would you take offense if I said that about your color?"

"As a matter of fact, yeah. It's not the same. I am black. I can't—" He came to a hard stop.

"You can't what?" I pressed. "Change what you are, who you are? Well, Mr. Harkins, neither can I."

He held up his hands. "Lady, I give," he said and backed off. "I didn't mean to offend your politics."

"You didn't. You can't."

He shook his head and I watched him go, typing on his tablet. I still didn't think he understood. It wasn't politics. It was about survival. He wasn't offering to help, he was offering a crutch. It wasn't a way to heal, it was a way to continue on as a cripple. Because even if we got through this thing his way, I'd still have, in my head, the idea that if I fell, the government would be there to pick me up. That was not how I was raised and it was not what I believed about myself or about this nation. Whatever part of this country you lived in, whatever stratum of society you were born into or rose to or fell to, I believed that you were responsible for yourself. Otherwise, whatever you achieved was not really an achievement, it was a dependency, a lark, a whim; not a fierce need, not a real risk. It was like riding with training wheels and calling yourself a biker.

That was not how societies grew. It was how they stagnated or fell.

I had been through rough patches in my life—the worst of them was what brought me down here to Nashville—but I had never faced a situation like this, where I had somewhat limited savings, all kinds of potential liabilities, and no clear path to tomorrow. I didn't know how long the insurance company would take to cover my loss—or how much of the loss they intended to cover. I also didn't really have anyone I could turn to for advice.

Those were the negatives, I thought. *What about the positives?*

I had come to Nashville to run a deli. I did that. I learned the business fast and had used my financial training and instincts to build on what my uncle had left me. I had good credit, I had a damn good staff, and I had me. I also had one other thing: nothing else on the horizon for as far as I could see.

So where did all those plusses leave me?

Uncertain and standing still on the street, neither of which was a place I was accustomed to. It was time to do *something*.

I turned to my left and started walking in a gathering rush. I was still uncertain. I still didn't know where to go, exactly. I couldn't decide whether to retreat or to attack—who and what, I had no idea.

But at least I was no longer standing still.

Chapter 7

I decided to just go somewhere else.

As I walked down the street to the parking garage, I felt a little bit of freedom but a whole lot of uncertainty. Despite my chutzpah with Harkins, I was scared down to my toes. I didn't want help, other than whatever insurance I paid for and was thus entitled to. Whether that was principled or independent or stupid, I couldn't say. To find out where I stood on my own, I decided to go see my broker, Alan Zebeck, who worked at a storefront agency on Charlotte Avenue. My cell phone was in my office and, to Alan's credit, when I stopped at a phone booth to call the deli voice mail, I found a message from him asking me to stop by. I had no opinion of the man. Alan was my uncle's broker and, although we had spoken on the phone, I had only met him in person once, when he came to the house where I was sitting *shiva* after the funeral. He was a heavyset guy, about five-six, balding, with a lisp. He had a senior partner, Steven Rapp, who was out of town for my uncle's funeral and whom I did not meet today.

Alan came out when the receptionist/secretary/partner's daughter Hilary told him I was there. He was dressed in a snug-fitting sports jacket. He gave me a warm hug and a sincere smile. He was heavier than he was when I first met him, a little more bald, but otherwise unchanged. I followed him into his office, where he already had my file open on his desktop. He did what it seemed to me a good insurance agent should do: he told me not to worry about anything, that he would take care of getting the property assessed quickly and would see that recompense was made. He was evasive when I asked for a ballpark figure. I would have been too, but I had to ask. Then he asked about injuries and it hit me that he wasn't enquiring out of concern for the staff.

"They're going to sue me, aren't they?" I said with awful realization. It was as if I'd walked into a pie that someone was just holding, waiting for me.

"It is likely they will sue you for physical injuries and psychological trauma," Alan said. "So, I suspect, will every patron who was in the dining room and more than a few passersby."

I wasn't naïve but I was still shocked.

"If it was an accident, they will charge you with negligence," he went on.

"It wasn't," I said.

That surprised him. "Then they will say you neglected to have reasonable security measures in place, that hostile acts by disgruntled employees or customers or enemies of customers is the new normal."

"But you can't foresee everything, and even if you could the cost of attempting to prevent it—"

"Don't tell *me* about the absurdity of it all," he said. "When your uncle took out this policy he was concerned about hot grease splattering on a cook or a busboy slipping on chicken fat. He had me write those very concerns into the policy, as I'm sure you know. The last thing he added was blue ice falling from an aircraft through the ceiling."

Blue ice was frozen toilet water ejected on occasion by aircraft. Typically, it vaporizes in the atmosphere. Sometimes it does not.

"You know, I understand the stuff that constitutes traditional workplace hazards," I said. "But this is idiotic." What was even more idiotic was that I was angry at my staff and customers and no one had even done anything yet.

"Be glad you're covered," he said with rabbinical finality.

"I am, but it's like I just told someone from the city buildings department, I don't like the way things work."

"It's the swinging pendulum," he said, still playing the part of the cleric. "A hundred years ago, people died in workplace accidents and the employers sent a wreath to the funeral—if that. It will come to center again."

"How? How do you get away from this *fachadick* mess?"

He snickered.

"What?" I asked.

"Your uncle used to say things like that. Hebrew words."

"It's Yiddish," I told him, sounding snippier than I had intended. I wasn't angry at him but at the system of which he was a part.

"I see," he said, though clearly he didn't.

"Hebrew is a Semitic language. Yiddish is from the German."

"I did not know there was a difference," he said. "Good to know. To answer your question, we all get away from binds like these when states put a cap on damages."

"How likely is that?"

"As likely as a cap on medical expenses," he said.

"So—nothing personal—but insurance companies raise rates to cover this stuff, the so-called victims benefit, and we go deeper into a world where everyone's *tuchas* gets powdered by me."

He nodded gravely. I was sick inside. If Lenin weren't glued to that glass coffin in the Kremlin, he'd sit up and clap.

"But here's some advice," he said. "There's nothing we can do about the system, so it's best we get ready to look after our own tookasses."

I appreciated the effort but here was another *goy* who couldn't do a guttural *ch*. At least Alan's heart was in the right place. So was his brain, which was good for me. I was already gnawing at my own insides but at least I had an advocate. At least I wasn't alone.

"Hey, what about getting back inside?" I said. "There are things in my office I need, like my cell phone."

Alan went to his computer, accessed a file, and printed out two letters. He signed one and handed it to me.

"The first one, the signed one, says the corporation—you—are fully covered against injury to you," he said. "The second says you abrogate all right to sue the city and its representatives if anything happens to you. If they want to retain these, that's fine."

"You have these ready to go?" I asked.

"Those and every convolution and contortion," he smiled.

I asked if I could check my e-mails and he graciously allowed me to use his desk. He left the office.

There were the usual business e-mails and a few from concerned restaurateurs . . . plus one that had just arrived from Candy Sommerton:

I tried calling and texting; no answer. Can you meet me at my office asap?

I wrote back:

No interview.

She replied:

No. More important.

I thought for a moment. I wasn't eager to see her but I was curious what could be more important than an interview to the interview queen. Plus, it was something to do. I said I would be there in an hour.

The rest of the e-mails could wait.

"Anything new?" Alan asked when I walked out to the reception area.

"Nothing," I replied. "Is there anything I need to do, anything need filling out?"

"It's all on file," he said. "I just plug in the data. Most of what I need will be in the police report."

"Thank you."

"I hope you're going home to rest—though it doesn't look like it."

I smiled. "I'm not from the resters."

"Your uncle wasn't from the resters, either. He burned himself out."

"I know. But I also think music did that. He wanted that more than anything. When it didn't come, I suspect he kind of gave up."

"He still played at the deli now and then."

"I know, but that's not the same thing as having your tunes on the radio."

"I guess not." He studied me for a moment. "What's your dream? Not the deli—?"

"No. The deli is—I don't know. A 'pit stop' sounds dismissive, but it's a good enough description for now. Why?"

"I guess I'm asking if you want to rebuild," he said.

"I don't know. Why? Is there something you aren't telling me?"

"Not really. It's just going to be a long road and the money is the same, more or less, whether you reopen or walk away. It's just something you might want to consider, if you have your eye on a different path."

He sounded sincere and his advice was sensible. I thanked him for the counsel and told him I'd think about it. And I would. I'd see how I felt when I wasn't suddenly obsessed with the idea that some shyster could actually get hold of my staff and convince them to sue me.

I don't remember going back to the car. Which probably meant I shouldn't have been driving at all. I tried to focus on something positive, like the fact that I wasn't still in the deli basement and I was alive, that the air I was breathing was clean. But when your life revolves around a group of people—your surrogate family—their absence, their injuries, and a theoretical adversarial relationship works unhappy, unwelcome wonders on your mood.

I concentrated on wondering what Candy Sommerton could want. It had to have been about either the cell phone video Benjamin had taken or the shots her cameraman got before the explosion. If so, why call me and not the police?

Or maybe she had and they were waiting for me, I thought. Maybe there was something incriminating on it, like I'd mixed horseradish with farfel and caused the explosion. She wanted to make sure she caught my arrest on video.

Candy's television station was located on Knobb Road, about sixteen miles west of the insurance office. I had been there once, not long after I arrived, to do a roundtable show on some noon broadcast about the importance of food to Nashville. It was an instructional experience. I was ostracized from the get-go by the awful silence that followed my opening remark, that without food, many Tennesseans would perish. I learned on that show, and from the e-mails I got over the next few days, that Nashvillians had a different sense of humor than I did. It didn't help that I felt like the odd woman out talking about white fish and chopped herring among all the homegrown chefs.

The building was a boxy affair, functional, with a reception area in the glass section off the parking lot and everything else—two studios— housed in big red brick. There was an Action Van with a satellite dish and an older Action Station Wagon parked out front. There were no police cars. I hadn't really been expecting them.

Candy was waiting for me in the lobby, her coral lips unusually pouty, her hair once again in its natural state of overteased. She was pacing and, upon seeing me, intercepted me halfway through the door. She took me by the arm as if she were about to sell me the bridge I used to live near.

"Come here," she said urgently. "I need to talk to you, in private."

As if I had a choice. She half walked, half tugged me to the van, opened the door, and went in before me.

"Slow down. My knees aren't working so well."

"Sorry," she said as we went inside. "I'm a little worked up."

"Noticed."

"This is—big. I think. Maybe."

I had never seen Candy so agitated. She shut the door hard behind us and we sat on two plastic swivel chairs before a modest console on the driver's side of the van. I sat still, slumping to stretch my legs; I was tired and my various cuts stung from the perspiration of our little jog. Candy swiveled.

"Did you ever meet that guy Benjamin before today?" she asked.

"No. Why?"

"Because neither Washington nor I can remember having seen him before the explosion," Candy said. "And my cameraman remembers everything that goes on in front of his lens."

"Benjamin said he was in the bathroom."

Candy shook her head. "Washington remembers someone else coming out of there and no one else going in."

"It's possible you missed him. I was there and I saw Washington moving around a bunch."

"It's possible," she agreed. "What's not possible is that 'Benjamin West' does not show up anywhere on the Internet. Not this one, anyway. There are plenty of others."

"Did you check his restaurant?"

"No," she said. "I wasn't really listening to all that."

I thought for a moment, remembered the business card he gave me, then rose a little so I could get his card from my back pocket. I held it toward the light of one of the monitors, which was tuned to an afternoon cooking show, *Olive's Oven*. I had done her show. Olive Boyle was a short, perky, pushy fiftysomething who looked thirtysomething due to twentysomething different facial alterations. She usually wore oven mitts because her hands looked like the rippling sands of the Sahara. I turned my attention to the card.

"Here's your answer," I said.

Candy leaned toward me and I showed her the card.

"His name is not spelled W-e-s-t but W-e-s-z-t," she said.

She typed it into a laptop that was plugged into the console. And there he was, just as he had said, listed as one of the two owners of GAB. They had a menu online but did not do takeout because, according to the site, "We cannot then maximize the temperature and plating of your meal."

"Crap," was all Candy could say. "A Quasimodo."

"What?"

"A bad hunch."

I didn't know which was more surprising, Candy making a politically incorrect reference or Candy making a literary reference. I also wasn't sure if she was ticked that she had lost a potential Big Story or was embarrassed to have called me there for no reason. Whichever, it was probably time to go. Once again, I didn't know where—just somewhere. I started toward the door.

"Wait," she said. She grabbed my arm.

Here it comes, I thought. The interview pitch. The way I was feeling, that was going to get her a long string of what-fors. I watched like a fencer on guard as she planted her feet on the rubber floor to stop swiveling and faced me.

"I just want to talk to you."

"Don't ask," I warned.

"Not an interview—just help me out."

"How? And also—why?"

"Woman to—"

"No, Candy, that's not going to do it," I said, hard and with an exclamation point. I was way past the age and era when sisters banded together for mutual protection. My former husband had a girlfriend during our marriage. She didn't look out for me. My father's ladies didn't give a damn about my mother. I didn't think my staff would sue or not sue me based on gender. I turned back to the door.

"What about this?" she said. "I need this story."

"You have it. You got the video Benjamin shot, the on-scene report. What more could you possibly want?"

"Actually, Gwen, the stuff you just mentioned makes the whole thing worse."

"How is that possible? You scooped everyone!"

"It raised the bar for the next report. It's

like . . . like a director who wins an Oscar, then has a flop. It would have been better not to win in the first place."

"Oh, please. Stories like this are forgotten in two or three days."

"Not this," she said. "There are a lot . . . well, a lot of angles."

"Uh-huh. Who live and dies. What happens to the deli. Who sues me."

"Never mind the details, Gwen, it's *news.*"

"It's also my life and I don't want to help exploit it."

"That depends on how the story is told," she said. "How it's spun."

If I hadn't just come from the insurance agent, that comment might not have gotten any traction in my brain. But it occurred to me, as much as I hated the thought, that having an ally in the press might not be a bad idea. That is, if I could trust Candy to stay on and remain a friend. I didn't feel sorry for her plight; I felt sorry for mine.

And then—I felt it rush in, like a cold winter wind. The rationalizations. Even if I didn't like the kind of stories Candy told, as a rule, journalists and the Fourth Estate were a good thing. If they didn't push for the truth, who would?

But Candy is different, I reminded myself. *She zooms in on tragedy and suffering and stays zoomed in.*

Yet people watched it, I reminded myself. That didn't make it news, that didn't mean I had to participate in the process, but as much as I hated the thought of it, I might need that platform one day soon.

"What do you want?" I asked, mentally kicking myself as the words came out. I figured I could at least go that next step.

"Thank you, Gwen!" she gushed.

"Hold on—it was just a question."

"Right. Right. I want to get back down there," she said.

"I don't have any say in that."

"You have more than I do," she said.

"And even if I did, why would I do that?"

"Because I'm begging you."

"Again, why? It can't be for just another day on top of the news cycle."

"It isn't," she said. "Just hear me out. Remember a few years ago when one of the tabloids was all over the John Edwards love baby story?"

"Kinda."

"The tabs broke it, they had access, they were all over it. They tied it all up and got it into a courtroom. The paper was almost nominated for a Pulitzer for that. Quite an achievement for a supermarket rag."

"*Almost* and *nominated*," I said. "That's a lot of qualifiers."

"But they were in the arena, fighting," Candy said.

"For what? A fool's errand. Where is the tabloid today? Where's the credibility?"

"They didn't capitalize on it, agreed," Candy said. "The thing is, how long do you think I'll be able to do what I'm doing? I'm already

Botoxing. I don't want to be like Olive Boyle, lifting my face till my socks are earmuffs."

That got to me. For the first time since I'd met her, I felt that Candy was being sincere. More than that, she sounded scared. I'd been there too.

"What exactly do you need?" I asked—warily, tentatively, not at all ready and willing to commit.

"Video, that's all," she said. "You can take it, that doesn't matter. I need pictures from inside, downstairs—something to show that I'm really plugged in. Something to get the attention of the national media."

"I don't know if I can get into the basement."

"Okay, fine, then whatever you can get me," she said. "I can do the setup out front then and cut to whatever you shoot with a voice-over. I'd owe you big-time, Gwen."

"That's not why I'd do it, if I did it."

"I know. But I don't have anything I can offer except an IOU."

I didn't know how to respond to that. I didn't want her to owe me anything—except maybe courtesy and respect. But if I expected that from her, I was likely to be disappointed, despite her sincerity now. So I didn't say anything. I just left and told her to get me a fully charged cell phone and then to meet me at the deli in an hour. She pulled one from a jack in the console of the van and handed it to me. I hoped it just happened to be there and that she wasn't figuring on playing me successfully.

I would tell the police I needed to get stuff from the office . . . which I did. I would shoot Candy's video from there, get some shots of the kitchen and the hole in the floor and the work going on there. It would probably be a useful record for me to have as well, for the insurance company.

But there was also something I wanted to check. The way the events played out, Benjamin *should* have been the last person to use the restroom. The classic toilet seat up-or-down test might not be conclusive, but something else might.

Chapter 8

If I didn't remember the drive to my insurance agent, the drive back to the deli was just the opposite. It had a hyper-real quality to it. Zebeck and Candy had gotten my mind focused and it stayed that way.

It was toward the end of golden time in the late afternoon when I reached the deli. The orange light and long shadows created a warm, homey tableau that I did not feel. That hurt because for as long as I'd been down here, whatever the season, whatever my mood, whatever the stresses or challenges of the moment, that light was like an old comfortable blanket over me and my adopted city. Today it felt foreign, like I was just a visitor here. My anchor was barricaded by several layers of police tape.

I walked up to the officer standing out front. He was a rookie, a sweet kid, but he knew me and I knew him. He always ordered oatmeal with sliced banana. I showed him the two letters from my insurance agent and he got a quick okay from a sergeant to let me in. I was grateful that Harkins wasn't around to get in the way.

I went right to my office following a dust-free path worn by the comings and goings of workers. There was a fine coat of grayish powder over everything else. It was like a science fiction movie where someone emerged from a fallout shelter and found everything eerily frozen in time and dusty. My cell phone was on the desk. I blew off the dust, which billowed and fell like a firework. The phone still had some juice. I used a marker to black out the cell phone light. I put the charger in my bag, which was plopped on the floor, then accessed the video camera function on the phone. I held it in my palm, face out. Candy had said she wanted the images to be moving and bobbing, not static. A cinema vérité look would make the viewer feel they were there, getting a true insider's look at my poor, ruined deli.

They would be inside, all right—inside the deli but not inside my head. To me, the deli where I had basically lived for more than a year and a half was as foreign as the street. All the electricity was off, save for work lights that were powered by a pair of generators near the Dumpster and strung around the blotch-shaped crater in the kitchen. A hazy cone of ivory light was coming from down there as well. But Murray's Deli itself was a dead husk, unwelcoming and unfamiliar. There was no warmth in the trappings, no trace of me or my uncle Murray or the staff in the dining area, just a muddy orange-gray where the light came through the front window and fell on the dust.

I lingered outside my office to give Candy her money shot of the pit. There was a thin cloud of dust and the workers all wore masks. It was miserably depressing and I turned away. I got some personal items from the office—photos, documents, my laptop—and the cash from the register and went to the bathroom. I checked the towel in the dispenser. It had not been used. I looked in the trash can. There was no toilet paper; it was as clean as when Luke had emptied it. Unless Benjamin had flushed the paper or wiped his hands on his pants—and men did do that, I knew—he hadn't washed his hands.

Or he wasn't in here and had lied about it. Why?

I thanked the police for letting me in. The kid at the door was very sympathetic and said he hoped that things worked out for me somehow. It sounded like he had heard more than I had but I didn't ask. He had a natural empathy. I didn't want to turn that into suspicion and regret by grilling him.

I returned to the parking garage and my car. I turned off the camera and sat for a while . . . and then I just started crying. Actually, it wasn't "just." It had been building ever since we fell down that rabbit hole and the few tears I'd spilled hadn't released most of the pressure and sadness. I was just becoming aware of additional bruises on my thighs, on my palms, everywhere that had taken part of the impact. Muscles were sore in my neck. And my hysterics didn't start out as crying, it started out as a sick, sick laugh; I actually wondered if I should consider suing the Murray's Deli Corporation. If that wasn't a comment on a *farblunget* system, I don't know what was.

The sixty-two-year-old manager, Randy, must have seen me on the closed circuit camera. A thin man with a thick gray moustache and goatee and an incongruous white suit—he was a livestock auctioneer until his skills were no longer required—Randy came down on his little electric golf cart, which puttered softly in the concrete cavern. He was a relic of the vanished South in other ways too. His Colonel Sanders look and scrupulous good manners instantly evoked a bygone age.

The man pulled up to the driver's side, got out, and rapped on the window. I rolled it down.

"Hey, Randy," I sniffled.

"Hello, Ms. Gwen. Forgive the intrusion, but you want to come to the office for a shot or two or three?"

I smiled at him. He was earnest, his bushy eyebrows so steeply arched they were almost vertical.

"I can't," I said. "I have to drive."

"Going once. I'll have Phil give you a lift."

Phil was the valet for nonregulars and people too lazy to walk down and get their own vehicles.

"I think I just needed a complete collapse," I said.

"Going twice. A drink can help. I know. I've done it."

"I think I did okay on my own," I grinned.

"You still having it? You want privacy?"

"I think it's over." I waited a moment, looked around as if I were waiting for a sneeze. "Yeah . . . I'm done."

He grinned crookedly. "Sold to Gwen Katz. You northern folks are strange."

"So I've been told."

"See, I can't turn things on and off like you just did," he said. "Couple weeks back, I saw a cat get run over here—squashed flat and I still can't get it out of my head."

"That's not something I'd forget, either."

"No? What about the kid who bullied me back at the school privy in Kingston?" he said. "I watch his Facebook page, know where he is at all times. I promise you, Miss Gwen, one day I'll get him."

"What are you going to do, put his head in a toilet?"

Randy's smile broadened. "I knew there was a reason I liked you. You got some rebel in you. One day that is exactly and precisely what I intend to do."

I hadn't been entirely serious, but Randy was. It was refreshing; you knew where you stood with the guy. Not like Harkins or lawyers or even me and my staff. What was really upsetting, I suddenly realized, was that because I was anticipating lawsuits, I was reluctant to go to the hospital. Nothing had happened, but I was already circling the wagons and I didn't want to look at Luke or the others, especially my two injured employees, and have that front and center in my head. I was going to have to go there, I *wanted* to go there—but it was awful to feel this way about it.

After making sure I was really okay—he ducked to window level and examined my eyes like I were a pig on the block, and I mean that in a good way—Randy scooted away and I sat a moment longer. There was a call on the cell phone. I smudged off the black marker with my thumb as I checked the number. It was Candy. I answered, told her I got her footage but that the battery was probably too low to send. I said I would bring the phone back to the station. She said she would prefer to meet me at the deli since she had to do the live broadcast from outside before cutting away to it.

"It has to look like I'm really in there," she said.

"I'm in the parking garage, level two," I said. "Meet me there."

"Why there?"

I looked around. "Because I feel safe here."

"In a bunker?"

I looked around. "Yeah. I guess so."

She said she was on the way. She also thanked me. That was like lemonade in the desert. Just goes to show you never know where a much-needed lifeline is going to come from.

I sat and waited until she arrived, my thoughts all over the charts. Nothing new; just fears sharpened by the passing minutes. When Candy arrived—with a new camera operator driving the van—she spotted me and literally bounded out. I gave her the phone through the still-open window, and as she looked at the video on the phone, her smile blossomed like a sunrise.

"Honey, I owe you," she enthused. "I know you don't approve of what I do or how I do it, but woman to woman, person to person—I appreciate this."

I shrugged. "Y'know, there are vegans who think I'm a criminal."

She looked with open surprise. She didn't realize that I had found a way to thank her for what she'd done for me without actually thanking her. She took my power cord, plugged it into an outlet in the van, and uploaded the video to her computer. She returned the phone with a smile and a hand that squeezed mine. Again, that was something I needed.

When she left, I put myself in motion. Not to the hospital; not yet. I drove home, fed my two cats, and got in the shower. I stood there, just letting the spray pour over my head, and was amazed at how much gunk collected on the floor of the stall. I grabbed the shampoo and washed my hair not once, not twice, but three times. The rest of me was pretty clean by the time I got to scrubbing it, which was a good thing; it would have hurt rubbing all the bruises and cuts. I pulled off the water-soaked bandages and applied new ones with first aid ointment. I had put my dirty clothes on the hook behind the door, but now I gathered them in tight-fingered fists and jammed them in the wastebasket. I wished I could burn them and all the thoughts the shower couldn't wash away. I felt better physically and, from experience, I knew my psyche would probably follow slowly, kicking and screaming to a better place.

Dressing in a monogrammed white blouse and black slacks, I knew what I had to do next: give my psyche a push.

Baptist Hospital is a massive complex covering nearly forty acres. The centerpiece is a massive stone building, ten stories of clean lines and a lot of glass. Visiting hours were nearly over but the gal at the reception desk was a regular at the deli. She knew me, knew what had happened, and she let me up to see my people. I crossed the lobby and ran into Luke and Dani as they were leaving the elevator. Seeing them was discomforting and strange. The fight-or-flight feeling that had been burning in my gut, the lawsuit crap, got pushed aside. The two looked alarmingly tired and pale—paler than usual, anyway.

"How are you?" I asked, looking from one to the other.

I was trying to sound warm and comforting but I did not get a good vibe back. Both seemed surprised to see me.

"It's all broken," Dani said.

"What is?" I asked.

"Everything," she said. "A.J. is, like, in this coma and Thom is crying even though it hurts to do that."

"Is A.J. really in a coma or is she medicated?" I asked, looking to Luke for an answer.

"She's got things in her arm—," Dani said.

"Dani, which is it?" I said a little impatiently.

She started a little at my tone.

Luke stepped forward protectively. "It's not a coma," he said. "She's sleeping. They took tests, I think an MRI, and now A.J.'s resting in bed. We waited for information but visiting hours are over unless you're family. A.J. Two is still up there."

"A.J. Two is messed up," Dani said. "It all is."

"It's going to be all right," I assured her. "We'll get through this."

"Not me," Dani said. "I'm done."

"Girl-pie, hush," Luke said.

Luke glanced from his girlfriend to me to the front door and hugged her tighter. I had been watching him during our brief chat, even when I was looking at Dani; that was the only time he had looked at me. Either he was numb or suffering post-traumatic stress from being blown down to the basement or he simply did not want to engage.

"Excuse us," Luke said as he moved around me, his arm still around Dani.

I got in the elevator, sick to my *kishkes* over his coldness. Reflexively, I held the door for a tall, muscular figure in a white bodysuit, a blue mask, blue trunks, and a blue cape that reached to just below the padded knees. They were a little worn and I tried not to imagine why he had those on.

He didn't so much enter the elevator as flounce in, like the improbable offspring of a bull and a gazelle.

"Captain Health thanks you!" he announced in a stentorian baritone that seemed to come from down around his knees and gained volume as it traveled upward.

"You're welcome," I said softly.

He rotated his finger around like it was stuck in a vortex before mashing the button for his floor. "Where are you going?"

I told him. He did another flourish and pushed the button as the door whooshed shut. He regarded me. "Is there someone in your circle in need of my services?"

"Yeah," I said. "Me."

"That's what I meant," he replied, his bravado surprisingly tucked away and a real man appearing. "You're Gwen Katz."

"That's right," I said.

"And before you ask, 'How did that amazing man know?' the truth is I possess super-percepto powers. Also, I have a Candy Sommerton app and saw her newscasts. And also, you have a big GK on your breast pocket. Put 'em all together—"

"Candy has an app?" I asked. I figured she tweeted, but that's as far as I'd thought about it.

"She does, and over the last two years she has done a great deal to spread the word about what Captain Health is doing to help kids get through tough medical situations," he said. "The community owes her a lot."

I decided not to debate the point; it took all points of view to make a world. "Is that what Captain Health does?" I asked.

"He does."

"I assume you have another identity?"

"You assume correctly, citizen," he said with a wink.

I smiled as we reached my floor. He got out with me and put his hands on his hips. I couldn't decide whether he was just into this or insane or both.

"But I cannot share that information with just any civilian," he said. "Gwen Katz, you look like you could use some—"

"No, I'm okay, thanks."

"—coffee."

The unaffected voice was back, still manly but sweet. That voice, like the unexpected words, was nice to hear. He removed his hands from his hips, locked them behind him, and winked. He might be a little nuts, but he made me smile.

"You're on, Captain Health. Where and when?"

"I have three kids to visit. One book reading, one balloon animals"—he patted a little pouch on his hip—"and one playing a computer game. How about forty-five minutes, in the lobby?"

Kids. Hence, the kneepads for kneeling at bedsides. I felt like a jerk. "Sounds good. Will you still be wearing . . . ?"

"Yes I will," he said. "Kids must not see me

except as the Defeater of Disease. I will make my astonishing quick-change in the Health-Mobile, which I have craftily parked out front."

I had to smile. The guy was committed. He was also cute. Beneath the owl-like mask, he had a strong Roman nose—not a lot of those in my past—and a solid jawline. He was probably a little old to be wearing the muscularly padded suit, but then it took age to have the kind of confidence to do what he was doing. He also proved that he was pretty good at what he did: cheering. This was the first time I'd felt my burdens lighten since the world and the deli floor caved in.

I turned toward the reception area. The staff was busy—some, distracted by Captain Health who waved and flexed his impressive muscles before getting back on the elevator—and I walked right by. I had no trouble spotting A.J.'s room along the corridor. A.J. Two was standing outside weeping.

I did not and could not know how this would go. What was the Old World saying? *Hope for the best, expect the worst.* A.J. Two was a smart young woman who had been scheduled to work that afternoon. She was also more reserved, more private than her outgoing mother. I didn't want to intrude on her moment so I stood to the side, her left side, and waited until she looked up. After a moment, she rubbed the sides of her fingers under her eyes and looked around. She saw me and drew a long breath before walking over. She always had good posture and she approached with her shoulders drawn back, her stride direct and strong. Her expression was neutral, however, her eyes were red. My heart galloped. It wasn't until she put her arms around me that I knew we were okay. She was slightly shorter than I and she cried big, heaving sobs on my neck.

I gave her a long moment, my hands cradling her head. Only when the crying subsided did I ask how her mother was.

"I thought I was hanging tough," the young woman said.

"You are," I assured her.

She smiled weakly. "Mom's unconscious—but she's still alive."

"Has she been awake at all?"

"Not that I could tell," the young woman said. "The doctors have her sedated and stabilized. She has three cracked vertebra, two broken ribs, and a mild concussion. Everything's been set and"—she started to lose it again—"my God, up close she looks like something out of a horror film."

"Don't think like that," I said. "This is all temporary."

She nodded. "At least she's got some color back. That's something."

"Why was she so pale? Did the doctors say?"

"Dr. Dundee said that it was from vascular constriction due to the trauma." She took out her cell phone, read from it. "They actually found that she may have something called Raynaud's disease which, if I got it right, basically scoops up all the blood to keep the major organs functioning and lets the extremities fend for themselves. That's why mom's hands and feet were—I mean *are*—always so cold."

"They haven't said anything about surgery, I'm guessing."

"Not yet. I hope not at all. They want to watch her for a while and they don't want her to move."

"Makes sense. Look, she's going to be all right," I said. "I know it."

"I've been praying for that, Gwen, for hours. First at her side with Luke and Dani and then out here, but I have a bad, bad feeling."

"You can't," I said. "Your mother would want you to be positive. She *needs* you to be positive."

"I know, but the way she looks, just lying there. She's always so vital. I don't know how to deal with that."

"We can figure it out together," I told her. "Come on. Let's go give your mother some good thoughts."

I took her by the hand and the young woman nodded, her tears a damp puddle on my shoulder. Together we walked to the room. The hand-holding was as much for me as it was for her. The door was ajar. We went in.

And something unexpected happened.

A.J. opened her eyes a smidgen and said, "Is that you, Two?"

For a moment neither A.J. Two nor I moved.

We listened to her mother's low but steady breath and the pulse of the machines announcing her vital signs. And then we heard it again. She spoke something small, breathy. We sprang into the room with such suddenness that I was surprised A.J. didn't scream.

I let A.J. Two reach the bedside first. She dropped to her knees, looked into her mother's partly opened eyes. They were red and moist but they were present, alert. I thought of going to get a doctor but I didn't want to leave A.J. Two.

"Honey?" she said weakly.

"Yes, mother. *Yes!*"

"I thought—I thought I heard you crying," A.J. said. "Like you . . . like you did when you were . . . a little girl."

"God bless you, Mom." A.J. Two wept again. "God bless you."

A.J.'s eyes shifted slowly to me. It took a moment for her to focus and another moment for her to smile, albeit faintly. She shut her eyes, the smile still on her lips. My own eyes snapped to the life signs monitor. I had no idea, really, what I was looking at, but I wanted to make sure that wasn't some last moment of lucidity before death.

"I'm going to go tell the doctor," A.J. Two said enthusiastically.

I squeezed her hand supportively and then she ran off. I looked down at A.J. "Listen, you.

I'll take your tables till you heal. But don't expect me to do it forever."

Her smile seemed to broaden slightly, or maybe it was my imagination. Whatever, it was the second truly happy moment I'd had that day.

I got out of the way when the doctors arrived. Kissing A.J. Two and telling her I'd call her later, I dragged myself up the stairs to the next floor to give Thom the good news. My friend and manager was asleep so I didn't bother her. Instead, I took the pen from her chart and left a note on a paper napkin on her nightstand. That should boost her spirits. Apart from the bandages here and there and the fact that her shoulder-length hair was splayed under her head, she looked okay. I hoped that Jesus was beside her. I truly did.

"How is she doing?" I asked the nurse as I passed him on my way out.

"She had visits from several of her coworkers and also from her church group, which really raised her spirits," the young man said. "Everything the doctor has said seems to point to a good outcome."

That was an obfuscation if I ever heard one— and as an accountant and a woman, I've heard a lot of them—but I had to agree that Thom's color looked good and her breathing was steady. In the professional medical opinion of a dispenser of chicken soup, that did indeed point to a good outcome.

I was breathing easier. My soul was a little lighter.

Now it was time for coffee with a superhero. I had already been through my supercop phase with Grant; hopefully, a superhero would be a little more entertaining. Still, with my expectations low and kryptonite in my soul, I headed for the lobby.

Chapter 9

There was a time, in memory yet green, when a coffee date meant cups and saucers or, at the very least, Starbucks. There was an element of "occasion" to it, however slim, and a potential for flirtiness across a table. You could even tell a lot—okay, prejudge—by what a person ordered. I made a completely unscientific study before I left New York. Guys who got the fancy, sugary beverages tended to be superficial metrosexuals. Black coffee drinkers were intense. Espresso? Self-absorbed, always glancing at their cell phones, plus they were giving themselves a fast drink for a quick exit if necessary. Double espresso? Need I say "wired"? Tea? Contrarians. Iced tea? Sanest of the lot, interested, a good bet. Bonus points if they ordered a brownie or pastry and gave me half. Sharing is sexy.

But this one was new. Coffee with Captain Health was a thermos in the passenger's seat of his van.

"How did everything go up there?" I asked.

"Beautifully," he replied. "It always does. Not because of me but because of the kids. They so want to have a magical experience."

"So they do. Helped a lot by you."

He nodded. "I give them a little push. Their imaginations do the rest."

That touched me.

"I know this may seem a little weird," he understated as he poured the joe into a real mug, "but there's a reason for it."

I thought, *Because you're about to drug me and to take me to the Bat Cave for some unholy purpose?*

But I asked, "And that reason is?"

"In addition to being a superman, I'm superspoiled when it comes to coffee," he admitted. "I have a greenhouse on my property and I grow my own organic beans."

"No kidding? How long have you been doing that?"

"Four years and a couple of months," he said. "I wanted to start the day with something special for myself. This seemed to be it."

I wasn't expecting that. I also wasn't expecting the full-bodied flavor as I sipped the brew. He poured a splash of almond milk into his own cup, then returned it to the cooler in the back.

"You grow and food process your own almonds too?" I teased.

"I would if I had the time," he confessed.

I didn't take milk or sugar even with the bitter, watery *pishockts* sold at roadside diners, but I certainly didn't need any of that with this.

I would be eager and proud to sell it. If I had a restaurant, that is.

"Wow," I said after the second sip, which was just as good as the first. Then added, "Now that I approve, it's safe to take off the mask."

He chuckled a little self-consciously. "Thanks for reminding me. It's like sunglasses when you go indoors. It's such a part of me, after a while I forget I have it on."

"It's also safe to tell me your name," I added.

He smiled but he didn't speak until he had carefully rolled back the carefully modified ski mask revealing, in addition to what I had already noted, sharp cheekbones and short, curly blond hair. Not bad.

"Kane Iger," he said, showing a lot of teeth. They didn't sparkle under the lamp post in the dark parking lot, but they should have.

I sipped more of his coffee while I checked him out. Damn, it was good. The coffee. And Kane too.

"You take this gig seriously," I said. "I mean—you obviously stay in shape."

"I try, but I do that for me, not the costume," he said. "An hour a day of push-ups, crunches, working with a medicine ball. My coffee tees things up and the whole routine gets the day going right."

"I'm impressed," I said. "If I can get out of bed, period, my day has started right."

"I'm sure that's not true," he said. "I get the feeling you love what you do. Otherwise you wouldn't do it."

"Most of the time that's true," I said. I got a pang when I realized I wouldn't have that to do tomorrow and tomorrow and tomorrow.

"What do you do with the rest of your day?" I asked.

I was expecting him to revert to announcer-mode and say, *In his civilian life, Captain Health is a mild-mannered blogger . . .*

Instead, he said, "I'm a money guy."

"Oh really?" I said. "I was in finance back in—"

"No, no, I mean—I work at a bank," he interrupted. "I'm an assistant manager at UTON." UTON was the Unified Trust of Nashville, an institution that was supposed to go places when it was launched in 2006, but stumbled in the financial implosion of summer 2008. It took a government bailout to survive. "I'm not a port-folio manager or broker or anything sexy like that. Mostly, I handle loans."

"Residential or business?" I asked, trying to purge the embarrassment he apparently felt at being a step up from a teller. Personally, I didn't think there was anything wrong with that. The hours left him time to have a life and do good things.

"I handle residential loans, mostly," he said. "I like people. I like *helping* people."

"Obviously," I smiled, gesturing with the coffee cup toward the costume.

"It's nice to always try and find a way to say yes and at as low a rate as possible," he said.

Even though it puts them in debt to UTON, I

thought with the muscular cynicism of a New York investment banker. It also helps fulfill dreams, if the lenders are responsible, not like all the clowns who gave out mortgages people couldn't afford, leading to the events of '08. I had to bite my tongue really, really hard not to rain on his low interest rates.

"So helping people—is that how the alter ego started?" I asked.

He nodded. "It was about three years ago. One of my clients had a sick kid. We had this costume our ad agency had used for a promotion—Captain Homeowner. Kids would always stop to see this superhero guy at a mall. That made it easy for our guy to pass out flyers to their parents. I always had an interest in superheroes, I admit it, so it was kind of a natural for me. I didn't even have to change the *CH* on the chest." He pointed to the big yellow letters in case I'd missed them.

"Worthwhile repurposing," I said a little enviously.

"What about you? Sounds like you didn't repurpose."

"Not a bit. I just chucked everything in the nearest wastebasket and moved from New York."

"With or without knowing anything about the deli business?"

"Without. Outside of the cash register and being able to tell matzo from a toasted bagel, that was pretty much all I knew. But I'm a fast study."

"What have you figured out about me?" he asked.

That was surprising, hard and fast like a super-hero punch. It took me a moment to think and another moment to decide whether I should answer.

"You look good in your threads," I said.

He chuckled. "Thanks. I wasn't expecting that."

"You were asking something else?"

"Yeah."

I grinned, and stalled by drinking more coffee. That *had* been a little shocking of me. In New York, candor is a way of life. Here, silence is good manners.

"I haven't figured out anything else," I said. "But you seem to have a good heart and that is more important than the size of the chest it's in."

That managed to embarrass him even more. He was running one hand round and round the steering wheel like it was a throttle.

"You're a native Tennessean?" I asked, throwing him a lifeline.

"Nashville born and raised."

"Ever married?"

"Only to my work," he said. "This work, I mean. The bank is a job, one that I like a lot, but this—this is like a calling."

When people say they're married to their work, it always sounds like a cliché, a default excuse for being a rotten spouse or friend or sibling. From him it sounded genuine.

"What about you?" he asked.

"I was married, for real, to a self-absorbed and

deceitful former husband," I told him. "If the choice is being married to a guy like that or being married to work, I'll take work. Any work."

"Sorry it was so bad for you," he said.

"There's that, but I also learned a lot about myself, my priorities. It's like any education—it costs something."

"Still, I wish it hadn't happened to you. And on top of all that, you have to deal with this new situation."

"Yes, but it introduced me to you and to some great coffee."

"True, but I'm still ahead in that accounting."

Another sincere expression. This may sound strange but I didn't know how to handle this much kindness and empathy. I didn't even know whether to run toward it or away from it. I didn't for a moment imagine I could ever end up with anyone as provincial as Kane, however sweet he was. That said, it was nice to feel appreciated. I was also getting way ahead of myself, though that was par for me too. There was something—*something*—intriguing about a guy who was a little bashful in this setting yet was uninhibited enough to appear in a superhero costume, fit enough to fill it properly, and either confident or naïve enough to have approached a girl while wearing it.

"So here's a question," I said. "If I were to join you on your escapades, what would my superhero identity be?"

He seemed pleased with the question. "That's easy. Soup Queen."

"Why?"

"Because everyone knows chicken noodle soup is good for you."

Now I was blushing. And, of course, I covered it with a joke. "I'd've gone with Latke Lass or Matzo Maid. But that works."

"Captain Health is good at names," he said. "Cheering kids up with names is really my thing. I always come up with them bedside. Like the Shiny Avenger for kids undergoing chemo or Tube Titan if they've got an IV."

"I'm guessing they love it."

"They do."

"I'm not really up on what kids go for," I admitted.

"None of your own?"

"Zero population growth for me," I said. "I don't need to mess up more than one life."

"You're being hard on yourself, Gwen. You shouldn't be."

"It's what I do. But enough about me," I said hastily. "So, Captain. You've got a Health-Mobile. I assume you also have a Health-Cave?"

"Over on Beech Avenue," he said. "I keep my Captain Health physique by running around Reservoir Park."

"I haven't been there," I said provocatively.

"They close at night so I do three circuits in the morning before I go to work," he said.

Closed at night. So—no park by moonlight. I turned my attention to the coffee. If he wanted me to visit, it was apparently going to have to come from me. I sat there thinking that I was seriously out of practice. I couldn't remember the last time I'd waited to be asked home. It was a strange, unpleasant, very retro feeling. I wanted him to ask even if I wasn't a hundred percent sure I wanted to go.

His hand started working around the steering wheel again. "Say, I don't have any women's spandex, but if you want a homemade smoothie—"

"Sounds good," I replied, perhaps a tad too quickly. "I don't get to the southlands much."

"It's a pretty undiscovered spot," he said, finishing his coffee. "That's one reason it's closed at night. Still deserted."

"Good for muggers or lovers," I said.

He laughed at that, which was good; I didn't have to roll out my A-game, humor-wise. I wasn't sure I could find it after this day and I was starting to worry that I was not making sense since I was tired *and* a little nervous. But at least we seemed to be on the same page: getting to a private place to see what developed.

I finished my own coffee, spilling some on my black slacks out of first night jitters. Then I got into my own car to follow him home, and off we went into the night, leaving behind a bad day and hopefully not giving birth to a bad evening. The ten minute drive was full of strange palpitations which I hoped was anticipation or first night jitters and not post-traumatic stress. Though I was guessing that if I had to come apart with someone, Captain Health would be a good choice.

Kane lived in a newish contemporary that looked unimaginatively like a big lean-to. But the big windows showed a lot of stars, the modern furniture was just right for the setting, and the lighting was low-key just *like* a cave—so as not to interfere with his Blu-ray viewing, I learned, from a library that consisted not surprisingly of a lot of movies with the Rock, Jason Statham, and Marvel superheroes.

Kane disappeared into his bedroom to change. There were no photographs anywhere, which seemed strange. Then again, I wasn't entirely used to the online cell phone world. That's where a lot of people kept treasured images. There were several stacks of well-read comic books and mystery novels in the bookcase, some college textbooks, a few best-selling novels from a few years back—before the age of the Kindle—and no newspapers or magazines. I noticed a video-game system attached to the television. If you wanted to occupy yourself here, it was either a copy of the *Amazing Spider-Man*, TV, or a game called Halo: Combat Evolved Anniversary. I felt a little antiquated and out of it, not having even heard of something that had merited an anniversary edition.

He emerged in a civilian version of his costume: a tight-fitting t-shirt from the 2014 UTON half-marathon, Nikes, and a snug pair of casual slacks that looked very good on him. He had the slightly stiff gait of a thickly thighed weight lifter, but his earnest smile was what I noticed first.

My host did, as promised, make a mean smoothie, which he brought to the living room. We sat to watch a big dumb movie with Mark Wahlberg and Will Ferrell. After a few minutes, Kane slipped an arm along the back of the sofa and around my shoulder. It was an old move, a trusted move, and in this case a welcome and effective move. I had never had a muscular, beefy arm on me. In New York, you mostly found those in gay bars. I snuggled closer and he looked at me.

"You have such a lot of love to give," he said.

I didn't answer. I didn't agree. I always felt I had angst to give and issues to resolve. Maybe he saw something I didn't. That would be new and nice.

"You're being very quiet, mysterious," he went on.

"Just enjoying the moment," I assured him. I was.

"Well, from where I sit, you must be very, very special," he said with a nervous, pubescent-boy catch in that otherwise confident voice.

"Oh?"

"I'm looking at you and not one of my favorite movies," he said.

That, I assumed, was a very high compliment from this guy. He didn't, thank God, break the mood by asking me what my favorite movies were. I'm not sure he would even have heard of *Wuthering Heights*, which would have required more mood-killing explanation.

I smelled banana smoothie on his breath, which went just fine with my peach. And that wasn't just the restaurateur talking. We brought the two flavors closer and that was the last I saw of the movie. His kiss slid from lips to cheek to neck. Fortunately, the product in his hair was subdued by the scalpy sweat generated by the hot costume he had been wearing; there was more man than salon in my nose. We ended up on the floor where I discovered that the rest of Captain Health was as fit as that sturdy Herculean arm had been. It occurred to me, at some point between hitting the carpet and heading to the bedroom—in his arms, I'll have you know—that this was the first time in my life I had been with someone younger than me. That took some mental adjusting; that plus the fact that it would probably be more like that than the other way as time went on. Happily, I was able to shut Analytical Gwen down as we disappeared into the darkness.

My newfound friend was not the big-time lover Phil or even Grant had been, but the night was everything I needed it to be. Cozy, warm, caring, and restful. I woke with the sun blazing through one of the skylights I hadn't even noticed the night before and, dressing quickly, I made my quick good-byes while he was still drowsy. I jotted down my cell number on a pad in the kitchen. I'm not sure if I really wanted him to call, but what the heck, I was in that kind of mood so it didn't matter right then.

I felt pleased and I felt good and most of all I felt attractive as I took the drive of shame. It was a fresh, sunny morning inside and out. I went home, fed two ticked-off cats—who were overfed as a rule and had nothing to kvetch about, though being Jewish cats, that didn't stop them—made a phone call, and then got in the shower. That felt really good too. There were layers of "yesterday" all over me, and I wanted to face today as fresh as possible. I scrubbed as near as I could get to the pre-explosion Gwen, dressed in jeans and a button-down white blouse as if I were going to work.

I wasn't. I was going to have organic pancakes.

Chapter 10

I had called Benjamin Weszt's number when I got home to last-minute accept his invitation to breakfast. He seemed surprised and delighted to hear from me. I was glad. That might soften things a little when I told him what Candy said about not having seen him around. Because if he wasn't around, how did he end up in the basement? There was no way in other than the trapdoor staircase in the kitchen.

Now that my phone was recharged, I could check my messages. I did that before I left the house. There was a message from A.J. Two that her mother was basically the same as she had been the previous night: moments of dim alertness but mostly sleep. The doctors were pleased, she said, that her mother had not gotten worse.

Well . . . of course. I would have been more pleased to hear that she had gotten better.

There was nothing from the staff about Thomasina, nothing from my insurance guy, nothing from Detective Bean, and nothing from

Kane—which did not surprise me since that was my track record with men. I refused to let myself get paranoid, like I was being shunned for legal reasons. I just wasn't used to being so cut off. For all I knew, the staff was feeling the same thing, that I wasn't looking after them. Or maybe they were just giving me time and space to deal with the disaster. Who knew?

God, how we can be our own worst enemies!

The bed and breakfast was a big antebellum house with a colorful garden on three sides and a lovely patio with vintage swinging chairs all the way around. It was, as advertised, "A Little Bit of Gentility."

Parking was in a long, curved driveway on the side. I pulled in and wobbled a little on knees that not only were still raw but got a little bit abraded the night before . . . from when I dropped off the sofa onto the carpet.

Breakfast was a buffet set on a long period sideboard in the den. Guests filled their trays and sat in the vintage armchairs that were arrayed throughout the large, sunny room. Benjamin and Grace were just coming down the staircase, looking at their cell phones. We were the only ones in the room. Benjamin definitely looked cleaner than he had when I met him, a pocket handkerchief short of dapper, wearing a starched white shirt and tailored plum-colored sports jacket and black trousers; Grace looked pretty in a pale yellow sundress. There was still something familiar about her that gnawed at me.

There were cheek-to-cheek kisses, after which

we went to the sideboard, Benjamin insisting I go first.

"Did you manage to sleep?" he asked as he followed Grace along the sideboard.

"As it happens, I did. You?"

"Yes. It was an exhausting day," he said.

"How's the room?"

"Very, very comfortable and quiet," he said.

"These old homes are just so exciting," Grace enthused. "We don't have anything like them in Southern California."

"But we don't have a Grand Canyon," I pointed out.

They laughed. We sat in a pinwheel array of armchairs, the sturdy wicker trays in our laps.

"I confess I was surprised to hear from you," Benjamin said. "But pleased. We really wanted to know how you were doing, how your staff is."

"I saw them last night and there's no change as far as I know," I said. "I'll go back to the hospital later this morning to see for myself. I also had to go see my insurance agent and I had to get things from my office. Oh, and I saw Candy Sommerton. The reporter you were kind enough to help."

"You didn't seem to get along with her," Benjamin said.

"I don't, really, but there was something she wanted to talk to me about."

"Anything interesting?"

I had some pancakes before continuing. "She said that neither she nor her camera operator saw you in the diner, in the bathroom, or anywhere else until we all met in the basement. And yet," I went on quickly, looking at Grace, "I could swear I saw you somewhere before yesterday. I just can't place where."

There's "awkward" and then there's *shpilkes*, a level of discomfort expressed by the amount of disgust one puts in the word. Judging from the way the couple stopped eating at once and sat frozen for several seconds, this was heavy *shpilkes*.

"How odd," Benjamin said when he found his voice.

"Which part?" I asked.

"That they didn't see me," he said. "I was there."

"Yes—you remember, I had the gefilte fish. We talked about it."

The woman was right, even if she did say the word as though it ended with a "t" and not an "uh."

My eyes became searching little slits. They shifted from Grace to Benjamin. "How did you know their names?"

"Whose?"

"Newt and Raylene?"

"I heard them later," he said.

"You weren't near them. I was looking in that direction. You two came from the other side."

"That's because we were taken to an ambulance there," Benjamin said. "Really, Gwen—what is this?"

"I don't know," I admitted.

"She's searching for answers," Grace said

charitably, looking at Benjamin, setting down her tea cup and laying a hand on his. "It's totally understandable."

He nodded. I looked back at her. I caught her in profile as she turned back to me.

"You did have the gefilte fish," I said.

Her eyebrows dipped and her look said, "What?"

"I saw you," I told her, flipping through images in my brain. "But not yesterday. Two or three days ago."

"No," she smiled, then hid behind her tea cup.

"We weren't here," Benjamin finished her statement.

The mood in the den had changed. Moments before we had all been warm and cozy among the big nineteenth-century furniture with its mist-green dandelion patterns, plates filled with hot, traditional food. Now they'd been busted, I could see it in their expressions, and things had frosted a bit. I had seen Grace in the deli, not looking quite like this, but she was there. I used a pair of mental spurs to urge my brain to greater action.

"Dark hair," I said to the woman. "You had black hair."

"Don't be—"

"Silly? Thom was on a break and I was on the register when you left. Let me see your sunglasses."

"I don't have any, Gwen."

"Coming from sunny California, Bubeleh, that story is stuffed derma."

Benjamin had deflated visibly when Grace said that. She was not quite the lying improviser he was.

I set my tray on an end table to my right. If they tried to get away, I wanted to be free to tackle them. I picked up a slice of toast with preserves and bit off the end.

Just then Elsie Smith wandered in. The fifty-something owner, wearing a frilly apron and a benign smile, looked us over.

"Is everything all right?" she asked. Then she saw me. "Oh, hello, Gwen. How are you, dear?"

"Peachy," I told her, holding up the toast.

"That's apricot," she replied, trying to be helpful. "I made the spread myself. It's the same recipe as my great-great-grandmother used."

"It's delicious," I told her.

"I want to say, Gwen, I feel awful about what happened. You'll let me know if there's anything I can do?"

"I will," I assured her.

I wanted to say, *Use your body to block the stairs so these turkeys don't bolt,* but I smiled—with both eyes still on my breakfast companions, who were eating mechanically and showed no sign of imminent departure—and told her we were all good. She dipped her head solicitously, like a great lady of the South might have done, and gave us the privacy she must have noticed I wanted. Or maybe she wanted it; tough to say.

Benjamin broke the fast-forming ice.

"Is there a Mr. Smith?" he asked.

"Deceased. That's all I know. Don't try to charm me and don't change the subject."

"Whatever you think, Gwen, it's not what you're thinking."

"What am I thinking, Benjamin?"

"That this is related to what happened. To the explosion. It's not."

"What is it related to, then? How long were you in my basement?"

He hesitated. Grace seemed uncomfortable. Her tray moved like it were a raft on rough seas.

After what seemed like an hour, with segments of time marked by my crisply crunching bites of toast, Benjamin said, "Ask your employees about this."

I stopped chewing. "My employees?" I said. "What do they have to do with this, whatever 'this' is?"

Benjamin was silent. He sucked down some scrambled egg from which steam had stopped flowing. He chewed soundlessly. If I didn't get some answers soon, steam would begin flowing from my ears.

"So you did know one or more of them before yesterday," I said, trying another tack.

Once again, neither of my hosts uttered a word.

I pulled my cell phone from my bag. "I'll just start calling them and asking."

"Don't," Benjamin said.

"Why?"

"Because that wouldn't be kosher."

"Hey, don't throw my words at me in a bid for mercy."

"I wasn't being patronizing," he said. "I was—well, it's like a reporter who swore to protect his source."

I was getting angry, not just at him but at my staff. And I wasn't even sure anyone who worked for me had done anything wrong—though now that I thought about it, Newt and Luke did seem to be uncommonly surprised when I came in early that day. Then again, for all I knew, this guy could just be *hockin me a chinick*—in other words, just bothering me to keep me off topic.

"So what am I supposed to do, just pretend you both didn't lie to me and that an employee didn't help in some way?"

"Why not?" Grace asked. "We didn't have anything to do with the explosion."

"So you say."

"I do say! Why would I lie about something like that? Why would we want to *cause* something like that? That is so very hostile!"

It would be too much to believe Grace was that stupid, even though she was young and blond with one of those nasal high-pitched girl voices that every young woman on earth seems to have embraced. Still, there was a chance the question might be sincere.

Regardless, I'd had enough game playing.

"Okay, I'm going to up the ante," I said. "I won't call my people but I will call Detective

Bean and ask her to find out why you were—what, casing my restaurant?"

"You mean, like criminals?" Grace asked indignantly.

"Just like criminals," I said. "You may not have caused the big bang, but you were up to something no good. So which is it, Grace? Do you talk to me or do you talk to the police?"

"You can't threaten us like that," she sputtered. "You won't be able to prove any darn thing!"

"*Au contraire.* Unless you slept in your car, and didn't charge a meal—which I think you did, because I remember you signing left-handed, now that I think of it—I can show you were in Nashville. Hell, I can go ask Elsie when you checked in—"

"All right!" Benjamin snapped. He forked a section of sausage into his mouth and set his tray aside. "All right. We'll talk."

"Honey," Grace said, "let me. Gwen, we read about the deli online and were thinking of buying the place. That is why we were 'casing' it, as you put it. And . . . we were going to promote one of your employees if we did."

"Promote them to what?" I asked impulsively.

"Manager," she replied.

That left out Thom, since she was already manager. And she never would have hurt me, no how, anyway. I looked at Benjamin. "So you were checking out the *basement* of the deli. For what?"

"Space," Grace said. "And vermin. It was due diligence so we would know how much to offer you."

"What made you think the deli would be for sale?" I asked.

"Isn't everything, for the right price?" Grace asked. "I mean, you were in finance. You know money. Isn't that true?"

She was perilously close to stereotyping me but I let it pass. There was a lot more about her story that ticked me off.

"So you took it upon yourselves to bribe an employee to get a look at the place?" I said, not quite believing it.

Grace nodded. I tore a slice of toast in half and started chewing as I glared at her.

"The basement," I said again.

"That's right."

"Tell me. Do I own that building? Surely you checked before looking into this."

They were both silent. Then Grace said, "We did not check that. It did not matter. We were interested in the business, in the goodwill you have built up over time, not in the structure itself."

"Why the *farkakt* wig?" I asked.

"Because you are *very* sociable," Grace said solicitously. "You talk to repeat customers."

"We've been to other restaurants around the country and proprietors don't have your people skills," Benjamin said. "We're going to scope out a few more here: Suit and Thai, The Curried Lamb—I'll bet we don't find anyone as interesting as you."

"Uh-huh. And you won't find anyone who asks probing questions like these."

Grace nodded. "That's a boon and a speed bump."

"Great name for your memoir, which you can write in prison."

Benjamin's mouth twisted. "You'd ruin one of your worker's lives over a little harmless snooping?"

"Me ruin it? You put them up to it, they made the choice! How the hell did I become the bad guy?"

"By virtue of acting like you're the SEC and this is an IPO," he said. "You're not, it's not. Let's just call it a poorly conceived way of doing business. We can roll it back. I can help you get back on your feet."

"God, that's the last helping hand I'd want!"

"Because you're thinking emotionally, not rationally," Benjamin said.

"Again, my fault. You have a real talent for *ungepatchked* thinking."

I hoped my sneering tone made the definition "messed up" clear to them. I finished the toast, picked up my coffee cup, and took a slug as I sat back and looked from one to the other. Grace and Benjamin, Benjamin and Grace. They were not stupid. So why would they do this thing like a pair of *moisheh kapoyers*—backward?

No, I didn't believe their little chronicle, but I had nothing to take its place. I was about to say that when my phone beeped. It was Dani. My *kishkes* burned when I saw the caller ID, like someone had turned up the gas on a range.

"Hi, Dani—"

"I didn't know who else to call," she sobbed.

"What's wrong?"

"It's Luke," she said. "He left here real angry."

"About what?"

"I don't know! He was up most of the night, not saying anything, just staring at the ceiling. He got up his usual time to go to work, got dressed, and when I asked where he was going he said he had something to do."

"Did he say what?"

Dani wept a moment, then told me.

I left the bed and breakfast without saying good-bye.

Chapter 11

It was a heartbreaking scene that greeted me when I reached the deli.

I parked in the street, leaving just enough space for traffic to pass, and ran to the door. There was no police officer outside and I knew why.

Luke was inside trying to go to work. He was standing by the cash register, his back to the door. The tall, skinny officer from out front was behind him and a burly engineer from the Department of Codes and Building Safety was in front of him. At the moment, the engineer was blocking him with his body. Luke was standing there arguing, gesturing. I couldn't hear what my busboy was saying but I could just imagine. This was clearly not the time to question if he was involved with Benjamin and Grace.

"Hey!" I said jovially as I walked in.

Everyone turned.

"Gwen, thank God!" Luke said. "These two

shmucks are trying to tell me I can't come to work today!"

"The thing is, Luke, we're not working here today," I told him.

He looked at me as though I'd told him his box turtle had escaped. "What are you talking about?"

"Look behind you. We're . . . renovating."

He turned. He just stood there, still and staring.

Growing up, I had always thought of post-traumatic stress as something that was the purview of the military. It wasn't. After the World Trade Center attacks, people from all social strata, young and old of all nationalities, went to pieces. Not just that day but in the weeks and months that followed. A lot of New Yorkers still look up at low-flying aircraft and their hearts speed up with a fight-or-flight response. I didn't suffer the same way. Though I worked down the street and the attacks shocked and sickened me, they didn't surprise me. My extended family was all about Israel and its survival and I was raised on news reports and firsthand accounts of terror attacks and war. Besides, since before the Spanish Inquisition, Jews have been more than a little paranoid. I haven't exactly made a secret of my guardedness.

Hope for the best, expect the worst.

I was unhappy but I was in survival mode. I had the tools to function, to plan, to poke around for information. Luke and the others did not. This was how the disaster affected him: denial.

Luke snapped his head back in my direction. "Thomasina . . . A.J."

"They were injured," I said. "They're in the hospital."

"Dani wasn't here . . . she's all right."

"Yes. You left her to come here."

He nodded. "Right . . . right. Crap. It happened. I didn't imagine it."

"You did not," I told him.

I looked at the engineer and cocked my head toward the kitchen, letting him know it was okay to go back to work. He seemed dubious. The Semper Fi and MIA stickers on his hard hat suggested he might have had more experience with this sort of thing than I did. But I knew my employee and felt I could deal with this. He left.

I stepped around the cop to stand beside Luke. The officer left my busboy with me. I took Luke by the arm and walked him to one of the dusty tables. Luke looked around the dark diner, looked at me, then looked down.

"Someone—me—has not been doing a good job on these tables," I said. "She ought to be fired."

"What am I doing?" Luke asked.

His hands were in his lap. I scooted my chair around so I was beside him, laid a hand on his. "You're trying to deal," I said. "We all are."

"Am I? I thought—I mean, I was lying in bed thinking about the basement . . . then I thought, like, *You dreamed that,* and I had to get to work." He looked around again. "Dani asked me where I was going and when I told her, I couldn't understand why she was crying. Now I do."

I squeezed his hand. "I can't quite believe it myself, Luke. But we're going to be okay. We're going to fix this."

"How? The kitchen is wrecked. *We're* wrecked."

"One step at a time, that's how," I told him. "We get our team well again. Insurance works on rebuilding. We figure out some way that I can give everyone some money so you don't have to go to work somewhere else."

"You would do that?"

"I would and I will. I *have* to do it because we're family."

Either Luke was genuinely moved by what I said or else it was just the little push he needed to go over the edge. Whatever the reason, he began to cry. He put his head to my shoulder and released heaving sobs. I felt the little boy in him emerge, scared and helpless, confused and grateful. Fortunately, I was only scared, and not as much as he was, so I was able to offer comfort and some strength. It wasn't fair. I could walk away from my life down here; the others could not. If I didn't put this place back together somehow, then that day, that hour, the way the sunlight looked outside the door, this particular street and location—they would always be vivid and pain-filled triggers. Worse, whenever Luke looked at Dani, it was possible he would see the lady who worked here and not the lover and friend who was in front of him. And that would cause everything to cascade back.

I saw a shadow on the floor and turned. Dani had arrived. She leaned her bike against the frame and came in. The police officer turned to address her but he caught the imploring look I shot him and held up his index finger, the universal sign of "*You've got one minute, lady.*" I was grateful for that. It wasn't the digit I typically got, and no, I mean the thumbs-up or -down sign from my staff when they needed help.

The sun made Dani's facial piercings shine in the dim light of the diner. With her pixie haircut and pale skin and the way she glided across the floor, she looked like a fairy from a Disney cartoon.

I nodded and smiled a little smile to let her know everything was okay. I whispered in Luke's ear that Dani was there.

He nodded into my neck, lifted his head as though it weighed as much as a bowling ball, and blinked at her.

"Sorry if I worried you," he said.

She smiled sweetly as she neared. "You did a little, banana bean, but as long as you're okay—"

"Yeah, I am. Thanks to the boss."

"You give good nurture," she told me with uncommon earnestness, ignoring our usual boss-employee formality and hugging my neck.

"Thanks. But I think you're the one he really wants and needs."

I said that loud enough for Luke to hear. The couple reached in front of me and locked both hands and moved away so that Luke could stand and they could hug. If I were a Talmudist and into symbolism, I would describe this as a moment of regeneration. But I'm not. There was still a long, long way to go. Still, it was a welcome change from all the destruction, alienation, and suspicion.

I gave them a moment, then reminded them that the place was presently unfit for habitation.

"We have to go," Dani said.

"This is where we met," Luke replied.

"I know. It will always be, like, special."

With that, the youngsters broke their embrace and walked hand in hand to the front door. I heard them agree to meet at home for a delayed breakfast. She promised she would make chocolate Pop-Tarts and Eggos. Luke *mmmm*ed. I remembered when I was a young teen and ate like that too, at the Royal Canadian Pancake House in New York. No syrup was too potent, no bacon too crispy, no portion too overwhelming. Then, my metabolism could handle anything and bupkes frightened my arteries.

I was alone in the dining room of my deli. The police officer ignored me. I thought about calling Kane, took out my cell phone, and saw that he had left me a message. My mind was held in a kind of reflexive, electromagnetic stasis between "that's sweet" and "don't smother me." I felt I should listen to the message first. For all I knew, he was calling to say he never wanted to see me again.

"Hi, Gwen," he said cheerfully in the message. "Just wanted to say how much I enjoyed the time we spent together. Hope to see you again soon. Take care—'bye. Oh, this is Kane. In case you didn't know. Captain Health," he added in his stentorian voice, followed by a laugh, followed by a good-bye in his normal voice.

He wouldn't get points for originality but it was a menschy thing to do. I probably would see him again, though with my penchant for attempting long-term planning, however often I failed at it, I couldn't imagine the relationship "going anywhere," whatever that even meant. The traditional relationship goals were crumbling as heterosexual couples just lived together while gay couples married and women were able to have petri dish kids at ages that postdated menopause. What was the point of even thinking about planning?

I got myself in motion toward the door. I saw the debris from the basement piled behind the counter: the utensils and cans and electronics that had been blown down to the basement. I decided that this was not the time to see what was salvageable. That was when I chanced to look back toward the office. The door was shut, which it rarely was during office hours; I only locked it at night because there was cash in the safe. I noticed something unusual. There was a tab of some kind sticking out from the edge, near the knob. I went over to investigate.

There was a thin, ragged remnant of silvery duct tape stuck to the jamb. I didn't touch it. Instead, I went to my desk drawer and got a pair of tweezers I kept for eyebrow emergencies. I plucked the tape off carefully, dropped it in a business envelope, and knew where my next stop was going to be: a place I hadn't visited since I broke up with Grant. The Central Precinct of the Metropolitan Nashville Police Department at 501 Broadway.

Naturally, every time I passed this way and saw that street sign I got homesick for the lights and craziness and hordes of gawking tourists of the Great White Way, told myself I was crazy to be here, and briefly resolved to go back to New York ASAP. But the sharp longing always passed, replaced by a dull one, just as it did this time. And lest you think I'm whatever the modern equivalent of a broken record would be about this—a "buffering" prompt?—I'm compelled to repeat, unapologetically, what we all learned from Judy Garland, that there's no place like . . .

I knew the desk sergeant, Nicholas Alexander, from my Grant Daniels days. He greeted me warmly, rising like a true southern gentleman, and offering his condolences for the "situation" I was facing.

"It isn't like our town to be this unfriendly," he said.

"I know that, Sergeant."

"Let me know if there's anything I can do to help out."

"I will," I assured him. Sgt. Alexander was like one of the cops I saw several times a week at the New York Stock Exchange, only Alexander's accent was southern instead of Irish. They both had that kind of earnestness that made you feel you could trust them with your life. Which was the point, I supposed.

Detective Bean was in. She came out and got me, brought me through a short corridor to the gunmetal desk that, along with several other desks, was the entirety of the precinct detective bureau. I sat in a thinly cushioned metal chair beside the desk and told her what I'd found. I presented the envelope.

"What's the significance?" she asked after peeking inside.

I explained where I found it. She nodded thoughtfully.

"You think it has to do with the explosion?" she asked.

"I don't know. Turns out Benjamin Weszt was in my basement before the blast."

"Oh? Do we know why?"

I explained that too. She asked if I thought it was an inside job. I told her I didn't think so. But what my inside voice was really saying was, *God, I hope not.*

Bean looked more closely at the scrap in the envelope.

"It's possibly part of a larger piece used to keep the latch from engaging," she said. "You can see some shredding here," she pointed along the side, "which looks to me like someone hurriedly tried to rip it away."

"Because . . . I was coming?"

"It's possible."

I hadn't thought of that but she was right. It was a quick, stringy break. I had arrived early. Benjamin's accomplice had worked it so my door wouldn't lock the night before. Whoever it was knew how I closed the thing, with a tug as I headed out, never checking to make sure it locked because it always did. He and his accomplice hadn't been expecting me, so one of them tried to remove the tape before Benjamin ducked into the basement.

What the hell could Benjamin have wanted in my office? Was he looking for files about the building? My lease agreement? Insurance costs?

"It'll take a few hours to get this through the system, since it's part of a probable crime scene," Bean said. "I'll call you when I have results even if we can't ID it."

I nodded listlessly.

"You understand that if we find anything, it may be necessary for us to talk to whoever it is . . . possibly more."

"In conjunction with the explosion, you mean?"

"That's right."

"Not about the office, per se."

"No," she said. "Any action in that regard would be up to you."

I was glad about that. As I left, I found myself doing something I rarely did: I prayed to God that the office incursion and the explosion were unrelated. Given their proximity in time and space, that did not seem like a reasonable hope.

Chapter 12

I stopped at the Salad Barre for lunch. It was run—no surprise here—by Josephine Young, a retired ballerina who got tired of explaining to people how she stayed so trim. The quote under the name said it all: "Don't eat pig, or like one."

The place had mirrored walls. There was a ballet barre on each with a plank on top that served as a table. That was standing room, announced by a sign written in Russian and given to her, according to a smaller plaque underneath, by the manager of the Kirov. The interior was filled with small round tables that were topped with old ballet photos and programs, all of them about the owner and her career in various companies around the world. There was no counter and no alcoholic beverages were served. As the menu itself declared, "There is no bar at the barre." Josephine and her female waitstaff all dressed in a leotard, tutu, and ballet slippers—pronounced *ball*et, emphasis on the first syllable as proper folks do. Meals were served on point. I wondered if half the customers came to see if a tray full of food ever dropped. Not that it mattered. She had a busy and growing operation. She was also one of the restaurateurs I beat for Best Mid-range Restaurant of the Year.

Josephine was a bony five-foot-six. Part of that was the result of her vegan diet, but some of it was also due to the fact that she was sixty-eight and her skin just hung a little looser than it used to. She made a great tabouli salad with tangerine slices and that was what I was in the mood for.

It was just after the lunch rush and Josephine welcomed me with a big, sympathetic smile and wide open arms.

"I am so, so very sorry," she said.

"Thank you."

I noticed, then, the tip of a placard with a wooden handle. It was upended behind the trash cans in the kitchen. I remembered Sandy's father, Alex, having said something about an anti-meat protest at his butcher shop the day of the explosion.

"Been out spreading the word?" I asked, dipping my forehead toward the sign.

She looked behind her and frowned. "That was my business partner, Ronald. I have a public face. I cannot afford to be an activist. The only time I protested was in my early twenties when funding was being cut for the Atlanta Touring

Ballet Association, which brought dance to schools. It was a very important project."

"Did you succeed in getting the money reinstated?"

She smirked. "Do these things ever?"

She was right. The only protests that ever made an impact were about civil rights. And the only groups that ever capitulated were those that stood to lose money by angering a consumer group. Ballet dancers were not such a bloc.

I ate my salad at one of the tables which, coincidentally, had a photo of Josephine and Ronald Carroll from the opening of the restaurant two years before. Ronald was a bald, thirty-something trust-fund brat and spotlight whore who cut a big fat arc through the local social scene. He invested in things that made him more money and, just in case things got slow, he involved himself in causes that generated him some heat, like loudly protesting the treatment of pigs and cows.

I often ate at places other than my own, though that was always a choice rather than a necessity. It was a crappy feeling. The place was more or less empty, just a few people chatting after lunch. I was huddled low around the ceramic bowl, which was locally handmade by Native American Chickasaws, yet another plaque on the wall said. My ancestors probably ate like this in the eastern European *shtetls*, protecting their meager meals from grabbing hands, ready to pick them up and run, in case the Cossacks attacked. I wondered how much of *that* was coincidence and how much was genetic memory.

There was a wind chimey–type of bell over the door and it tinkled as I was finishing my salad. I heard low male voices but didn't look up, which is why I hadn't realized that Democratic Mayor Louis Benedict Dunn and an aide had entered the eatery until Josephine said his name. Well, of course. He had to compete with Moss "Com" Post and his Eden Party. Where else would he go for a late lunch but to an organic eatery?

Josephine was all over the mayor, whose eyes were on me as I glanced up. His aide recorded the arrival on his cell phone; no doubt it would be on YouTube within the half hour, showing how Dunn was the sane green candidate. Truth be told, that was not something I disputed.

Dunn walked over and shook my hand. The cell phone was still recording. He said he was sorry and asked if there was anything the city could do to help. I remarked that he could kick Big Jefferson Harkins and the rest of the sluggish, inhibiting Department of Codes and Building Safety in their collective *baitsim*.

"Backsides?" The mayor chuckled.

"Other side," I said. "They come in pairs."

The mayor harrumphed and smiled uncomfortably and walked away, trailed by his flunky. I was pretty sure that remark would not make it onto the Internet.

The two men went to a table as far from me as they could get, while I finished my lunch and checked e-mail and phone messages. There was nothing from any of my employees. I would stop by the hospital after leaving here.

There was a text from Kane. He wanted to know what I was doing for dinner. I decided not to answer it yet. The way things had been going, who knew how I'd feel in six or seven hours?

I paid and said my farewells to Josephine.

"Gwen—you understand that, as much as I would like to help, I can't offer you my facilities to store or cook your food. I mean, if you were planning on doing takeout or something."

"Don't worry about it," I told her. "It's like a kosher deli. Vegan and meat don't mix here."

"You do understand, thank you. Just the smell of cooking chicken liver would—"

"Would make your customers sick. Of course." Odd that she chose liver.

We embraced, and I waved good-bye to the mayor. He pretended not to see me, being buried deep in meaningful conversation—though you can always tell when someone is avoiding you by the way their eyes don't move at all. I shouted a good-bye and, since he couldn't feign deafness, he waved and smiled and didn't bother to return to his discussion. Unlike his buildings department minion, this mayor had no *baitsim.* I drove to the hospital.

When I arrived, I felt like I'd been hit in the back of the head by a baseball bat.

A.J. Two was standing just outside the sliding lobby doors talking to Andrew A. Dickson III,

attorney-at-law. Dickson and I had once been
on opposite sides of a nasty property struggle.
Just the sight of him gave me a heaping of
umru—apprehension. He was about five-six,
bald, African American. Instead of his trade-
mark tan camel hair coat, he wore a navy jacket.
Dickson wasn't exactly an ambulance chaser, but
he was not averse to following whatever gurney
rolled from inside. I felt like making one of
those moves I'd seen in detective shows, where
you crouch real low and move between the cars
to avoid being seen. But then, I asked myself,
what did I have to avoid being seen *about*? And
didn't I just kvetch about not being seen by the
mayor? If they were talking about suing me, let
them.

I walked boldly up to the two. Their conversation died instantly, like a mouse in a snap trap.
I glanced at Dickson and then turned to A.J.
Two. Her eyes were dark and bloodshot. She
looked like she hadn't slept in two days. I quietly
asked how her mother was.

"She's still in and out of consciousness," the
young woman said.

"You should find out whatever you need to
know from the nurses, Ms. Katz," Dickson said.
"Now, if you'll excuse us—"

"Why?" I asked, firing him a look. It was the
kind of look I used to give my husband when he
was being a shmuck. Yet despite that show of
defiance, my stomach dropped as though I'd
swallowed a matzo ball whole. I didn't want to

add to A.J. Two's woes, but I wasn't going to let this guy, any guy, push me around.

"That is, frankly, none of your business," Dickson said in a voice that was silkier than his imported tie.

I looked at A.J. Two imploringly. "Don't do this."

She frowned. "Don't do what?"

"Don't talk to him. We're family, all of us."

"I know that, Gwen, but—"

"Ms. Katz, please do what you came here to do and leave us to our business," Dickson insisted.

"Don't interfere, Mr. Dickson," I insisted right back.

The attorney puffed a little inside his jacket. He reminded me of a burrito in a microwave. "I was about to offer you the same advice," he said. I turned physically from him. I was afraid I might kick him.

A.J. Two looked at me like the mask of tragedy. "Gwen," she said softly, "truly, this is nothing that concerns you."

"Then why did everything suddenly get hush-hush when I walked up?"

Dickson replied, "Because if my client's mother is awake, you will be speaking to her."

"Your client, huh?"

"That's right."

"And what if A.J. *is* awake? Isn't that a good thing?"

A.J. Two became agitated. "Dammit, Gwen, that isn't the point! We're discussing the living will she left behind and I don't feel like talking about it more than I have to, okay?"

Dickson stood there, his expression perfectly defining the word "smug." And I stood there— just barely, on legs that felt like freshly cooked kasha—perfectly defining the word "putz." I wanted the concrete to consume me, as the Sinai did the sinful Children of Israel. But God wasn't willing to oblige.

"I'm so sorry," I said to A.J. Two in a voice that was surprisingly strong and repentant. "Jesus, I'm sorry. I'm an idiot. God, am I stupid."

"No, don't do that," A.J. Two said. "Gwen, we're all under a lot of stress and you've taken on all of ours on top of your own. I know you were just trying to help me."

She was wrong about that. I'd assumed they were talking about suing me. I hugged her tight and walked briskly through the doors. Tears spilled down my pale cheeks. I was so mortified I didn't even want to be around myself. To find the last time I was this embarrassed, I had to go back to the second grade when I was playing the piano in an elementary school talent show and went blank on "Tomorrow" from *Annie*. To this day, I can't look at an image of that blank-eyed mop head without cringing.

That wasn't the normal you back there, I told myself as I walked through the lobby toward the elevator.

Or was it? Had I been getting crankier by the month, by the week, without realizing it? Had the stress of shootings and land grabs and everything else soured me? Had my staff been too polite to mention it? Was that scene outside the next stop on my descent from a moderately happy Wall Street titaness to what I privately thought of as a mindless organ grinder, chopping liver without enthusiasm?

Oy gevalt. Big-time.

But this is not the time to take an objective look at your life, I cautioned myself. *Deal with one little mission at a time. The next minutes are about Thom and A.J., not you.* Which is why I found myself praying that I did not run into Newt, Luke, or Dani while I was there. The cryptic exchange with Benjamin and Grace was still rattling around in my head. I didn't want to deal with that now, either.

Thom's nurse said she was asleep after a restless night. She was recovering but really needed to rest. I asked the young man to tell my manager that I'd been there. He said he would. I went to A.J.'s room. The nurse met me in the hall and told me that A.J. was still unconscious and sedated, but was stable and breathing steadily. I went into the room and choked up. She was breathing as steadily as one could with tubes *shtupped* up her nose. The bruises she had suffered on her cheek, forehead, and bare arms were ripe and ugly. Her daughter had done her best to brush her mother's hair and make her look presentable, but without her bright red lipstick and her brighter smile, without eye shadow and rouge, she looked like an ashen, broken thing. She reminded me of one of those zombies you see on TV.

I sat for a while beside her bed and lightly held her cool fingers in my hand. I moved a thumb along them, felt their texture, was alarmed by their stillness. There were whistling birds outside and chirping electronics inside—beautiful, innocent, taken-for-granted reality on one side and a hard-fought struggle on the other. But we *do* fight. A.J. would fight.

"I—," I began, then stopped. *This is about A.J. It shouldn't start with "I."* "I've been thinking about what we were talking about in the kitchen yesterday," I said softly. "You were glad you have a girl, not a boy. You said you know where your daughter has been because you've been there. Well, honey, you haven't been faced with the kind of situation she's in now. I'm begging you, wake up. Don't make her decide about taking you off life support. I won't make one of my usual smart-ass comments like, 'If you do that I'll kill you.' Get better. Go back to her. She needs you and so do I. So do all of us."

"That's the truth," a man said from behind me.

I recognized the voice. It was Newt. I gently put A.J.'s hand on the sheet, rose, and turned. I took in the "street" Newt, one I rarely got to see. The young man was dressed in gray sweat clothes and new Nikes. His dirty blond hair had been finger combed and his brown eyes seemed somehow darker than usual.

"Hey, boss."

"Hi."

He stood there awkwardly for a moment.

"Walked here," he said. "Figured I'd better watch my gas money."

"Good thinking," I replied.

He hesitated, then came in, circling to the bottom of the bed. There was something off about him. He was usually in your face; he seemed guarded. Yes, it could be the sight of his frequent nemesis bedbound and helpless. Or it could be facing me, and not because he was planning to sue.

"How are you doing?" I asked.

"Okes," he said, using one of his neologisms.

I walked toward him. "Glad to hear it."

"How're you?" he asked.

His question hit a stony face with disapproving eyes. "I want to talk to you," I said.

"All right. When?" He didn't ask why. Maybe he knew. Or maybe, like I did with A.J.Two, I was vaulting to a conclusion that had no validity.

"How about now?" I asked. "As soon as you're finished with your visit."

He looked at A.J. lying on the bed, her hair splayed on the thin hospital pillow. He walked over to her, kissed her sweetly on the forehead, then came back.

"I'm finished," he said.

I asked a nurse for directions to the cafeteria. It was one flight up. I took the stairs because I didn't feel like waiting for the elevator in awkward silence. Newt followed. It felt to me like we were heading up a scaffolding to an execution, maybe because things were going to be said that could be fatal to our relationship.

Newt must have sensed it too. He stopped suddenly.

"I can't," he said.

"Can't what?"

"I can't talk. I don't want to."

"To me?"

"To anyone," he said. "I just want to go back home."

I was three steps ahead. I walked toward him. "Why? You don't know what I'm going to say. Frankly, I don't know what I'm going to say."

"There is suckage in the air," he said. "I feel it. Why pretend? Things are never going to be like they were. I just want to go."

"Run away, is that what you mean? From what? You didn't have anything to do with this, did you?"

"Jesus, no!"

"Then what? Talk to me! Is it Benjamin?"

He looked at me like he'd just been shot from a cannon and didn't see a net.

"It's all right," I assured him. "He told me why he was in the basement," I said, taking a stab in the dark that Newt was the inside accomplice.

"He did?"

I nodded calmly, trying not to scare him off, so I could get at the truth.

Newt looked at me suspiciously. "What did he tell you?"

"That he was interested in buying the place and that someone let him in." I added, "Someone who may have left tape on my office door so he could go in there too and look around.

The police are analyzing it now, looking for fingerprints."

Newt's expression melted from frozen shock to unbridled laughter. It happened so fast, so unexpectedly, that it actually frightened me.

"Newt, what——?"

"They're gonna find my fingerprints!" he said. "And the good news is, at least I won't have to worry about getting a new job! The state'll give me one!"

"Why? I'm not going to press charges about letting that *schmendrick* in to look at the place."

"That's not what he did," Newt laughed. "Boy, I thought this would get me out from behind the grill and ahead in the world. What a dope. What a moron!"

He turned and started back down the stairs, steadying himself on the banister. I went after him.

"Newt, what did he do? What is this about?"

"You'll have to ask him," he said. "Really. I want to hear what he's going to come up with next."

I grabbed Newt's shoulder and pulled him around. "I'm asking *you*!"

As suddenly as the laughter had started, it stopped. "It's about a Hail Mary pass by me to get more responsibility, get away from that job behind the grill. I don't want to talk about it. Not to you, not to anyone."

With that, Newt wrenched from under my fingers, ran down the stairs, and kept going. I didn't know anything more than I had before yet, somehow, I liked it all a lot less.

Chapter 13

I drove to the bed and breakfast and wasn't surprised to find that neither Benjamin nor Grace were in. Benjamin also didn't answer his cell. Detective Bean called to tell me that there was nothing definitive found on the duct tape. I didn't bother to enlighten her.

I sat in my car outside the Owlet, watching the sun slowly sink and, with it, my will to move. I thought about Newt, how afraid and crazy he was. And he hadn't been down there with us. I knew he couldn't be responsible for the blast; I knew that. But the duct tape—

And then I wondered if I'd gotten it wrong.

Wouldn't I have noticed if my door didn't shut? I wondered. Assuming the answer was an affirmative, why was the tape there—unless it was applied *after* the explosion. No one would have a reason to close my door, but if they did—

Maybe it was one of the workers, the engineers?

But why? They had no reason to go into my office. They didn't have a reason to go anywhere near there, in fact. The plumbing in the building had been compromised so they'd brought a portable toilet to the courtyard, next to the Dumpster.

I had to figure this out, which meant going back there. I wondered if part of my return was an unwillingness to let go; better a dead deli than no deli. It was a sad thought, because it meant that I had nothing else to turn to.

Before going back, I checked my messages. There was a new voice mail from Kane, but it was from his alter ego:

"Captain Health is off work at four p.m. today and is offering to assist Ms. Gwen Katz in whatever activity she is engaged in. Should her plan include dangerous sleuthing, so much the better. For beyond aiding the young and ailing, there is nothing Captain Health enjoys more than righting wrongs and solving crime."

It wasn't weird, like the first time I'd met that persona; it was silly and stupidly irresistible. I called and got him on the phone.

"This is Soup Queen—a.k.a. Latke Lass a.k.a. Matzo Maid—and she gratefully accepts your offer to help her go a-sleuthing," I said.

"Excellent," he said, managing to drag it out to four syllables. "Where are you?"

"At the Owlet, but I'll meet you at the deli."

"Wait outside for me," he said. "There may be danger if you go in alone."

"I'll wait," I assured him, making a mental bet

that he showed up in costume. I gave myself even odds on that one.

I was wrong.

Kane showed up as Kane, but with a gleam in his eye that I had first seen at the hospital and not thereafter. He had been charming and out-going, which is why I ended up staying the night, but helping was clearly what his inner life was all about. I even found myself questioning how harshly I had judged him when he said he liked finding ways to give people loans. He really was about spreading joy and goodwill, even over the resistance of cynics like me.

He parked on the street a block away and got there before me, since I always went to the garage. I liked knowing my car was in a brightly lit place covered by security cameras. I didn't drive in New York, but I never understood those people who spent a half hour or more driving round and round looking for a parking spot when there were so many parking garages. Yes, they were expensive—but peace of mind was worth that to me.

"You thought I was going to appear in cos-tume, didn't you?" He grinned.

"I confess, I did."

"And I have to admit I was tempted," he said. "But I didn't know how that would play if there were cops guarding the place. I didn't want to make things difficult for you."

"I appreciate that," I said.

There was one police officer out front, but he was texting. He recognized me, nodded, and resumed what he was doing. There were no longer any engineers working inside. The structural situation had apparently been stabilized, even though the Department of Codes and Building Safety had been along to put in their two cents with a red UNSAFE sticker on the glass door.

I told the officer we were going inside to look through the personal stuff that had been hauled from the basement. He waved us under the yellow tape. Kane held it up so I could go under. I've got to admit, the gentlemanly stuff had an effect.

The deli was even more dismal than before given the late afternoon light. I went to the heap of items. The larger things, like the microwave, were sitting by themselves. The smaller pieces like ladles and cleavers were thrown in a stack about three feet high and six feet long. I used a broom handle to push things aside.

"What are you looking for?" Kane asked.

"Anything from my office," I said. "Someone apparently used duct tape to keep the door from locking. I assumed it was to take something out before or after hours. Now I'm wondering if it was to put something back in."

"Any ideas what?"

"None," I admitted. "But I'm not seeing anything here that came from my office. Nothing of mine personally and nothing corporate. Just metal and electronics."

Kane cocked his head toward the front door. "Security here isn't exactly airtight. Someone could have come in already and done whatever they intended to do."

"True," I said.

We went to my office. I took the flashlight from the desk and shined it around. Everything looked pretty much as it did the last time I was here. Kane took a Swiss Army Knife from his pocket and flipped out a built-in LED survival light.

"Nifty," I said.

"Never know when there will be a power outage or terror attack," he said. He shined it away from the desk, which is where I was focused. He examined the shelves where I had the various slipcase ledgers and corporate documents. "Check this out," he said.

I turned and looked at a spine where his light was shining.

"My uncle's recipe book," I said.

"Did you use it recently?"

"No."

"There's a drag mark in the dust on the shelf," he said.

Damned if he wasn't right. The shelf was forehead high for me, but he could see the scuff marks clearly.

I withdrew the book from the shelf. There was no dust on the top of the book, either. When I removed the fat elastic band, no fine gray powder fell from underneath.

"Looks like someone took it out and put it back," Kane said.

"Yeah. But why?"

"Are these secret?"

I shrugged a shoulder. "Yes . . . but if anyone was really dying to make my horseradish at home, all they had to do was ask."

"I'd bet that someone wanted to make more than horseradish—"

"*Loch in kup,*" I muttered.

"What?"

"It means I need this like I need a hole in the head. Could that be what they were all talking about?"

"Who and what?"

I put the book back and turned toward the door. I walked into the corridor slowly, thoughtfully. "A restaurateur from California was with us in the cellar, and claimed to be sampling all the local cuisine," I said. "Name's Benjamin. He just admitted that he was down there before the blast because he was looking the place over to make an offer. He said one of the employees helped him get in. But what if that wasn't why he was here at all?"

"Why else? To steal your recipes?"

"Exactly. He and his girlfriend, Grace, have a Tex-Asian restaurant already. What if he was simply planning to steal all my recipes and was downstairs to photograph the book, was making copies when the kitchen caved in. He couldn't have put it back like he'd planned with all the cameras and security around. So Newt helped him again—"

"Again?"

"He let him in before I got here."

"Bad boy," he said, imparting the mild phrase with genuine displeasure.

"Then, while we were trapped, Newt hastily ripped off a piece of duct tape and put it on the door so Benjamin could get back when the heat died down. The tape tore going on, not coming off."

"Where do you keep the roll?"

"Behind the counter."

Kane went to get it. "Not here," he said.

"Newt must have taken it with him," I said.

"He would have thought to keep the door from locking with everything else that was going on?" Kane asked.

"I guess so. Maybe he was hyper-scared. Maybe he was wondering if Benjamin was the one who caused the explosion."

"Is that possible?" Kane asked.

"Why not? Maybe he was planning to open a new restaurant here and wanted me out of the way."

"That's a lot of death and destruction to cause just to bring new cuisine to Nashville," Kane said.

"I guess, though it's probably no crazier than blowing up a deli to kill a mayoral candidate or any other reason I can think of."

Kane looked into the dark kitchen. "Still, I don't think these events are related, the theft of the book and the explosion."

"How so—," I started to ask, but resisted adding "Captain Health?" Kane was in full-steam-ahead crime-busting mode.

He stepped from the office. After checking to

make sure the officer was still busy texting, he shined the flashlight toward the kitchen.

"What have the cops told you about the explosion?" he asked.

"*Shtikl*," I said. "A whole lot of nothing."

"*Shtikl*," he repeated the word. "Is that releated to 'shtick'? A comedian's act?"

"Actually, yes," I said as we started down the corridor. "It's a little piece of a performance."

"Nice to know," he said. "I wish I had studied another language. You're very lucky."

I had never thought of it that way. I could get by in Yiddish, and it helped me to pick my way through German, though I wouldn't consider myself fluent. Still, he was right. I was lucky to have that resource in my head.

"You said you didn't think Benjamin and the explosion are related," I said. "Why?"

"Because there was no way of knowing what might have happened to him when it went off," Kane said.

"But he didn't expect to be down there."

"Correct. Don't forget, though, if something went wrong, he had an accomplice in the diner—his girlfriend. She could have gotten him out or made an anonymous phone call about the bomb."

"Good point," I said.

"Unless he didn't know about the bomb," he added thoughtfully. "She might have wanted him dead."

"That's . . . an interesting theory," I said. She hadn't struck me as the type. Which, of course, was why she just might be. "But then surely Benjamin would have suspected something. He's many things but not stupid."

"Does she pretend to be?"

"Maybe a little," I admitted.

"It could be she's fooled him," he said. "It's like Captain Health tells his children. We have to be strong and fight diseases because they never do any good. People are the same way. If they committed industrial espionage and coerced one of your people to help them, I wouldn't put anything past them."

We reached the kitchen. The back door was closed now and it was dark save for the small light from the flashlight. My God, this was a horrible thing to see, the tiles around the hole sagging inward, wooden beams visible underneath the floor on the far side, propping it up like it was a mine shaft.

"This isn't going to tell us very much," he said in a whisper as his light probed the darkness.

"How do you know that?"

"They cleaned everything up."

"What were you looking for?" I asked.

"Evidence of the delivery system," he said. "You know—a bucket, a briefcase, something like that. You can see where the bomb first hit."

"I can?"

"Look at how some of those tiles are a little melted," he said, using the flashlight to indicate the raw edges of the side of the hole nearest us. "The blast was somewhere around where we're standing and the heat was hot enough to melt the ceramic component of the tiles. That could have been what saved you."

"How so?"

"It took a second to melt. You slid instead of dropping."

"That's right," I said. "You seem to know an awful lot about this stuff. How do I know you didn't set the bomb?"

"You don't, nor I you," he replied.

"You think I tried to blow up my own store? And me with it?"

"I don't think so, but it isn't impossible, is it?" he asked. "Maybe you're in a deep financial hole so you get the insurance and get out."

He had a point. Whenever my father would read about a factory fire in the papers, he called it "Jewish lightning." The owners would simulate an act of God for a payday. The implication was that while anyone would take a risk like that, Jews were more inclined because of the profit motive.

"To answer your question," Kane said, "I took a couple of criminology classes in college. The stuff just fascinated me, the result of a lifetime of reading Perry Mason and Sir Arthur Conan Doyle along with Batman comics. That was before he was the Dark Knight, when he was still the world's greatest detective. I thought it might be fun to be a private eye, but my folks had other ideas. As what you might call 'white trash,' it was important for me to have standing in the community."

That made me sad. Then again, it was no different from all eastern European émigrés, who wanted something better for their kids than scrubbing floors and stocking grocery shelves, even if they had to force that choice on them.

"You want to stake them out?" he asked.

"What? Who?"

"The lovebirds," he said. "Benjamin and Grace. We should see what they're not showing or telling people."

"How?"

"See where they go, what they do."

I have to admit, the prospect appealed to me. Those two *fressers* from California had corrupted an admittedly corruptible employee with the promise of advancement in their corrupt world. That may not have defined "supervillain" in Captain Health's world, but it meant "rotten people" in mine.

"If you're serious, let's do it," I said.

"I'm very serious," he said. "I love doing this . . . with you."

That was sweet and a little oxymoronic. It reminded me of the *Bounty* mutineers who told Fletcher Christian they were proud to be with him after setting Captain Bligh adrift in a longboat. That sentiment ignored the fact that mutiny was a hanging offense. In this case, stalking was probably very, very illegal.

But so was industrial espionage. And blowing up a deli.

I wanted whoever had done this.

Chapter 14

Thinking that Benjamin and Grace may have seen my car when I was here—or peeked out to see it so they could watch for it in the future—we drove Kane's van to the Owlet and parked across the street. Darkness had settled in and we parked away from the streetlights. It was like an honest to God FBI surveillance . . . minus all the necessary equipment.

"The G-men used to just eyeball their quarry in the early days," Kane said as he poured me coffee from his thermos.

"Were there G-women in those days?" I asked.

"I suppose so," he said. "I'm sure they didn't do the same kind of field work, though."

"No, I'm sure of that. They were probably all Mata Haris."

"I'd bet they weren't all seductresses," he said. "Some were probably secretaries or scrub-women."

"Jobs where women would hardly be noticed," I said with a little bite.

"Well, yes," Kane said, pouring coffee for himself in a ceramic mug. "Isn't that the object of undercover work?"

He had a point.

"And I'll bet they had African American bootblacks and white men hawking papers or pretending to be lushes at bars," he added. "Anyone who wouldn't stand out. People who are ordinarily invisible."

"Makes sense," I had to admit. Sometimes feminism shouted louder in my ear than cold, sane reality.

"The only minority I ever belonged to was 'nerd,'" Kane went on thoughtfully.

"Were you oppressed?"

"Not really," Kane said. "Growing up, I wasn't big on sports or cars or any of the usual things boys are interested in. For book reports, I read novels about the Lone Ranger and the Shadow. I worked out at the gym, I ran, I swam, because I was determined to look like Batman. I was at least physically intimidating, so people kind of made a wide circle around me."

"Girls too?"

"Girls especially. They were very clique conscious. It was toxic to be seen with an outsider. My dad used to worry that I was 'queer,' as he called it. He tried to get me interested in watching football. I asked him how come his men in tights were any straighter than my men in tights? He couldn't answer that one."

"Pretty funny," I said. I looked out the window. "They could decide to stay in for the night."

"You said they're connoisseurs, right? They're going to want to sample what they can while they're here."

Another good point. Kane was pretty sharp at this detection stuff.

We sat silently sipping coffee. All was dark around us, quiet. Kane was a gentleman, didn't even put a hand on my knee, which both pleased and annoyed me. There's the dichotomy, right? No wonder guys can't figure us out; we don't know ourselves.

We chatted a little about people we knew in common—mostly my customers and his, which happened to include Elsie Smith of the Owlet—and finally the couple emerged. They were dressed for dinner, Benjamin in a sharp blue blazer, Grace in a satin sheath of the same bright blue.

"That's them," I said.

"I figured," Kane said. He watched them carefully. "Look—they're not holding hands, not walking arm in arm."

"They're not even talking," I said. "But it's more than just a business relationship. At least, that's what he said."

"If you can believe anything he tells you," Kane observed.

Benjamin took out his cell phone and started tapping on it. Grace did not look over. She was busy examining the gardens that lined both sides of the walk. Spotlights, hidden inside shrubs beyond them, threw a charming light along them and the cobblestone path. Grace paused to take a photo with her cell phone.

"She obviously likes the nighttime design," Kane said.

"They'll steal from anyone, anywhere, anytime," I added bitterly.

"They've already admitted that," Kane said. "We're here to find out what they maybe aren't admitting."

The couple went to their rented car. Benjamin did not open the door for Grace and went straight to the driver's side. Either she didn't approve of chivalry, they'd been together a longer time than I thought, or he just didn't give much of a damn about her. But before either opened their door, they had a conversation across the hood of the car and then apparently changed their minds about driving, and they headed down the sidewalk together—still not holding hands.

"So what do we do, follow them on foot or in the van?"

Kane was quiet, contemplative.

"Captain Health?" I said.

"Following them isn't going to tell us what we really want to know, is it?"

"I don't know. It was your idea."

"I thought we could learn something watching their body language," he said.

"We have. They're not as lovey-dovey as they pretend to be. That doesn't exactly make them unique."

"True, but their motives may be. Everyone loves a good romance. It keeps us from scrutinizing things too closely."

I wasn't convinced that it was as calculated as that. I thought back to how both of my big-time loves, hubby Phil and Grant, always made a show of putting an arm around my waist when we were at a party or with other people. That actually felt worse than being ignored, like I had value only as an accessory. When we were alone, I was like the pickle that happened to be on a plate. It could be the same with Benjamin and Grace—though, in support of what Kane had said, they weren't even married yet. Things couldn't have gone that far south already.

"So what do we do with that?" I asked.

"We check to see what they don't want us scrutinizing," he said.

"Whoa, hold on!" I grabbed his sleeve. "What are you talking about?"

He smiled, reached past me, and popped the glove compartment. He removed a large leather sleeve. "We're going to investigate," he said. He hesitated long enough to fold a stick of chewing gum into his mouth.

My grip had weakened and he slid easily from the driver's side door. I followed him quickly.

"Kane, wait!"

"Do you know what room they're in?"

"No," I said.

"Doesn't matter," he told me as he strode along the path. He hopped up the stairs to the patio and rang the bell.

I caught up just as Elsie answered the door. She had on her pleasant, neutral hostess smile. It stopped being neutral when she saw us.

"Well! What are you two doing here?"

"We'd like a room," Kane said provocatively.

Elsie blushed quickly and actually recoiled. "For . . . the two of you?"

"Good lord, no." Kane grinned, winking. "We were talking business, refi for Gwen's place. She mentioned that a friend is coming up with her husband to help her. Thought they'd make it a mini-holiday." He looked at me. "Did I get that right?"

"You sure did," I said through a big, phony smile. "That's Liz for you! Her motto is always try to turn a tragedy into recreation. Does that with funerals too. That's why they don't want to stay with me, even though I have a house. It isn't really a vacation, then."

My mouth was running like the Pamplona bulls. I couldn't help it and, worse, Kane seemed to be enjoying my distress.

"I see," Elsie replied.

"Anyway, Gwen said she'd check out the rooms," Kane said. "Possible?"

"Certainly," Elsie said, admitting us. "When are they planning on coming down?"

"That depends on what rooms are available when," I told her. "After they looked at your website, they decided they didn't want to stay anywhere else."

"How sweet of you all," Elsie said. "Well, come

on. I'll show each of the rooms to you, provided
no one is in. I don't think anyone is."

I suggested that we start with the four rooms
upstairs, since I knew one of those was where the
Californians were staying. We followed Elsie up.

"I don't know what I'm going to do when I
can't go up and down the stairs any longer," Elsie
said. "Maybe install one of those seats that rides
up the banister."

"Or maybe Captain Health can come by and
carry you," I offered.

"Who?"

"That's Kane's alter ego. He entertains children in hospitals, dressed as a superhero."

"How very thoughtful," she said. "Yes, you
could run into a phone booth at the bank—well,
maybe not a phone booth anymore but a broom
closet, perhaps—just like Superman, rush over
and assist me, then hurry back before you're
missed."

"The superhero's dream." Kane smiled.

We hit pay dirt with the first room. There were
three open suitcases, clothes on the bed and
hanging in the open closet, and two laptops
side by side on the desk. There were towels on
the back of the chair and over the footboard of
the bed.

"I apologize for the condition," Elsie said.
"They have requested that I not bother tidying
up in here."

"Young love," I said. "It functions wildly, un-
predictably, at all hours."

"That must be it," Elsie agreed.

I pretended to check the view while Kane moseyed about. We left quickly and went on to the next room. I had not missed Kane sticking the gum into the latch opening. That, not the latch, was what held the door shut. I also did not miss Kane backing out the doorway once Elsie took me into the next room.

"Where is Mr. Iger?" she said, looking around.

"He probably went back downstairs," I said. I leaned forward. "I have a feeling this sort of thing bores a lot of men."

"Straight men, anyway," she said.

"Right."

We looked at the other rooms, only one of which wasn't taken, though everyone was out for the evening. I hoped Kane had done his surveillance work quickly and was back downstairs since the tour took less than five minutes. We went back down and Elsie was visibly surprised not to find him waiting.

"He must have gone outside to use the phone," I said.

"Ah," Elsie replied. "Reception in here is regrettably spotty. Your friend Benjamin kept going outside to use the phone."

"Alone?"

"Yes. I don't think his lady is very much interested in his business dealings."

"How do you know they're business?"

"Oh, he's always so intense," she said. "Not relaxed, like he was with you. I think he is trying to buy property. That is such a brutal business."

"Probably more than any of us realizes," I said.

I thanked her with all the warmth I could muster considering that I felt as cool and sweaty as that pickle I mentioned earlier. I turned to go outside knowing damn well I wouldn't find Kane there. My heart thumped annoyingly as I went to the van and waited, hoping I hadn't made a mistake comparable to Yul Brynner chasing Charlton Heston through the parted waters.

I received a text.

"Keep talking to her, away from the stairs. I need to get down."

Without hesitating, I turned back. "Oh, Elsie," I said cheerfully, "there is one thing I wanted to ask."

"Yes, dear?"

"The flowers out front—I'd like to ask you about one of them. I'm thinking of growing it at home."

"I don't know about those," she said. "The gardener takes care of that."

"Right, but maybe you could ask him for me if I pointed it out?"

"Of course," she said as she got a shawl from the closet and came outside with me. It wasn't a brisk night, but she was a bony lady and pulled the shawl closer. I was sorry to make her do this.

I asked her about a purple star-shaped flower at the foot of the walk. I positioned myself so I could see the front door. Kane emerged quietly, walked to the side, and stood there in the shadows with his phone. We saw him when we turned back to the house.

"Ah, Mr. Iger," Elsie said. "You were so quiet there we didn't see you!"

"After libraries, banks are the second-quietest commercial institutions in the nation," he said.

"I didn't know that," I told him.

He grinned. It was a big, satisfied smile. I was eager to learn what was behind it.

Elsie stood on the patio and faced the street. "It's a bit chilly but a nice night. They usually are, down here, don't you think? I have only been north once but it was beastly. I went to Pennsylvania with the late Mr. Smith. It was about ten years ago, a family reunion." She made a face. "A bunch of Yankees. I never felt so out of place."

"I'm a Yankee," I pointed out. Some things you can't let stand, no matter how much you want to move on.

"I meant no disrespect," Elsie said. "But people can be good people, well-meaning people, and still have very, very little in common."

"But you married a Yankee."

Elsie smiled. "Lemmy wasn't a Yankee. Not really. He spent most of his adult life in the South, building roads. He understood our people, our values, the importance of the land. He knew you couldn't simply use eminent domain to pave over a farm that had been in a family for generations, you had to go around it. He knew that a hillside could not be blown up if it had significance to the locals as a traditional place of courtship or if it had been an outlook during one of too, too many wars fought in this country."

"Blown up?" Kane said. "Was he involved with explosives?"

"He wasn't—what do you call them? A demolisher?"

"Demolition experts," Kane said.

"Yes. No. He wasn't on that crew. He was a supervisor."

"How did he die, Mrs. Smith?" I asked. "If you don't mind my asking."

"In an accident on the job," she said. "A landslide when a detonator cap went off in a worker's pocket. The other man lost his legs but survived."

"That's awful," I said. "I'm so sorry."

"I had to fight for two years to get the insurance money that was due me," she went on. "A Yankee firm in Hartford, Connecticut. They had to do their investigations, you see. It wasn't enough that I had insurance on my husband's life and he was, clearly, quite deceased." She looked at me. "Did you have that problem with your restaurant?"

"No," I admitted. "It was a different situation. That was a will. I inherited the property. All I had to do was pay a share of the estate tax."

"Yes, well, I had problems with the estate too because there was no will," Elsie went on. "We were so poorly prepared."

The situation was unfortunate but Elsie was getting morose. And I was getting paranoid. I was waiting for her to say that the guy with the detonator cap was named Goldberg or the insurance agent was Horowitz. We thanked her for her hospitality.

"You will let me know, won't you?" she called after us.

"About?"

"Whether you will need a room."

"Yes—of course, absolutely," I said. I waved as I continued to walk.

"Worst continuity ever," Kane chuckled.

"I forgot. I tend to get caught up in the moment. What about you? Did you remove the gum?"

He stopped, gasped in horror . . . then smiled. "Of course. Captain Health is very, very thorough."

We got into the van. Before the doors were closed, I said, "I assume you found something in the room? You seem very, very excited."

"I did find something," he said. "A couple of somethings. First, a local cell phone number on a pad." He had copied it down and read it to me. It was Newt's.

"Okay. We knew that. What else?"

He produced a receipt. I turned on my smart phone, read the receipt in the light. "An off-the-rack cell phone."

"Purchased three days ago," he said. "For cash, I'm willing to bet."

"I'm not clear how this helps."

"An improvised explosive device, triggered by a cell phone," he said. "And just let your mind run for a second. Homemade devices include hydrogen peroxide, nitric acid, and nitromethane, still easy enough to get in very small amounts that don't raise flags. As for other ingredients, like pesticides and fertilizer—look along the path. They wouldn't even have had to buy that one."

"All of that from a sales receipt?" I said. "Seems a big leap."

"If we were trying to build a case before, maybe. But this is after. The bomb happened. A classic, terrorist IED. It could be that these folks were thinking of opening a restaurant here and didn't want the competition."

"Those still seem like pretty giant steps to me," I told him, switching off the light. I looked out at the street. "I still don't buy that they'd risk blowing up the kitchen with Benjamin down there."

"Why not? Certainly removes them from the immediate list of suspects."

"And what about planting the bomb?" I answered my own question. "A disguise. Grace used them to case my place. And they had the protest as a distraction. She could have been there while he was at my place. She rushed over in time to be seen."

"There you go."

"But even if it's possibly true," I said, "emphasis on the 'possibly,' what do we do with this? We aren't cops and we didn't exactly have a search warrant."

"True, but we can tip off your detective friend

that the receipt was in the office trash and have her take a legitimate look for the phone."

"The office trash?"

"He was there, wasn't he? In your office, replacing the recipe book."

"Yeah, but to be that stupid—"

"Maybe he plans to pin the thing on you. Maybe he's going to call them with an anonymous tip. For all we know, the cell phone is already there behind some books."

That sent a chill up my back.

"Wouldn't there have had to be a receiver phone in the bomb debris?" I asked. "Wouldn't Bean be looking for a triggering device already?"

"Possibly," he said. "There's only one way to find out. Call her."

He was right. But now that we were at this point, part of me recoiled against further action.

"What's wrong?" he asked.

"Part of me is insisting—pretty loudly, in fact—that I not get involved."

"Isn't it a little late for that?"

"Sneaking into their room isn't really—"

"No, I mean your deli was blown up, your people hurt, your livelihood seriously impacted, your hard work given a big flat tire. What part of your life is not involved?"

"That was passive," I said. "Couldn't be helped. This is aggressive. I'm mad at them because of how they suckered Newt. They're going to say I have a vendetta."

"And the facts will prove otherwise."

"What if they don't?" I asked. "What if Bean goes in there and doesn't find anything? I can't show her the receipt and my credibility goes down the drain."

"All valid points," he admitted. "If you want to defend inactivity, I mean."

That was a valid point too. "I should think about this," I said.

"He may toss the phone."

"How do you know he hasn't already?"

"I don't," Kane said.

"You didn't find it."

"I didn't have time to look. But I'm not sure it's the kind of thing you just dump in a trash can. Someone is likely to pull it out. You pack it in luggage where it won't raise any red flags, take it back to California, and lose it there. Do you want me to call?" he asked. "I will, if it helps."

I looked down at my cell phone. Was I being reluctant to get in deeper or was I having trust issues with Kane? It was silly, but I didn't want to lean on a man. Not after the way Grant inserted himself in things.

"No," I said, sitting back. "I have a better idea. Drive."

"Where to?"

"Just follow my finger," I said, pointing ahead. "I'll tell you where we're going."

Chapter 15

An argument could be made—and my brain was busy making it—that I was on my way to wrecking another relationship in its earliest, most improbable stages. Taking charge of this guy, pushing him around, supporting and then sort of disagreeing with his approach. On the flip side, I was a deli owner, not a private eye . . . despite my track record at solving crimes. These are decisions I shouldn't have to make. As a *balmalocha*, an expert, I was no *balmalocha*.

But, whether I asked for it or not, the responsibility had ended up on my shoulders. Yet there was a third option.

Benjamin and Grace had mentioned a few restaurants they wanted to visit. Only Suit and Thai was in walking distance of the Owlet. The place was popular with the business crowd during lunch, less so at dinnertime.

"Oh ho," spoke Captain Health as he looked in the big window, past the pulled-back curtains that looked like big neckties. "Intimidation by proximity. I like it. Show up, see how they react."

"Actually, I was thinking of something even more intimidating."

"Really?"

"Yes. I think we should confront them with what we've—*you've*—found and see what they do."

Kane was silent.

"My sense of it is they'd have five options," I went on. "The first three would be deny, deny, deny, followed by bribe and flee. What do you think?"

Kane Iger did not say a word. I only heard his deep breathing.

"I take it you have some reservations," I said.

"Some."

"Share," I said.

He reflected a moment longer, then said thoughtfully, "However they respond, we're not empowered to *do* anything. We can show up, which is innocent enough, and enjoy them squirming a little because—hell, because they're bad people. But everything beyond that is a matter for law enforcement."

"Even though the evidence—and I use that term loosely—is very, very weak?"

"It's enough to send up a flare," Kane said. "Then we can sit back and watch what happens. You walk in now, as you say, they will deny whatever you say. And we'll be asked to leave, having accomplished nothing but tipping them off."

I looked in at the couple. They seemed relaxed enough, professional gourmands who were really into whatever they were eating. They were actually connecting over the meal, making eye contact, sharing from one another's chopsticks.

The tease annoyed me. We had gone from bold to craven. Maybe Kane was right, but I didn't like getting dressed up with nowhere to go.

Kane must have sensed my frustration. He grabbed my arm.

"Let's call Detective Bean," he said.

I shook my head. "I still have credibility with her. I want to keep it. Plus—these guys hurt me. I want to go in."

Kane relaxed his grip. "Okay, but to do what, exactly?"

"I don't know," I admitted. "But I need to be in motion, toward something. I'm beginning to realize that's how I've done everything since I've been down here. Everything in New York was structured—the rules governing my work, the activities governing my downtime with my husband, the interaction with my mother that had boundaries designed to keep both of us away from the things that really bothered her. I'm not going to nurse bad juju anymore. I'm going to spread it around like *shmear* with chives. You coming?"

"Can we try a measured approach?" he asked.

"Meaning?"

"We go in, sit down for dinner, and see what they do before we charge over?" He smiled thinly. "It's what we in the South call a compromise."

That made me laugh.

"All right," I said. "We'll go in and just eat."

He looked at me skeptically. "You're sure?"

"I'm sure."

"Because last night, you warned me we were just going to make out and—"

"That was different."

"I agree, and I liked *that* result," he said. "If you create a scene in this place—those guys get to leave Nashville. We have to stay."

"I don't plan to create a scene," I said a little indignantly. "We're just poking the hornets' nest. A compromise, like you said."

I opened the door and he got out as well. By the time we entered the restaurant, I was so tired of talking and negotiating that I pretty much forgot what I'd agreed to. Not that it mattered. Benjamin saw us and did not react at all. A moment later, Grace looked over and smiled slightly before returning to her meal. We were shown to a table. There were several empty tables between us. Kane ended up sitting with his back to them. I was just too fast for him.

"You sure you want to sit there?"

"Oh yeah."

"Why, Gwen?"

"If I don't, I'll keep turning around and that'll be worse."

He had to concede the logic of that. He didn't understand the growing emotional storm but I knew that until I had someone to pin the explosion on, these suntanned *yutzes* were going to be the target of my displeasure.

We ordered. If you asked *what* I ordered, I

couldn't have told you. I watched them seeming to have a perfectly fine time while I was not.

"Relax," Kane said, taking my hands in his. It was only then that I realized I had shredded my chopstick wrapper into fine little sections.

"I can't," I apologized.

"You're not trying. Look at me," Kane said. "Into my eyes."

I made the effort. I looked. Then I looked past him at the happy couple.

"I've got to go over," I said.

"Gwen, you promised."

"I know. But if I don't stir things up, I'm going to blow up. Look, a few minutes ago you told me these guys might be bomb makers. I have to know."

"I also told you why we can't be the ones to confront them."

It may seem, at this point, that I qualified as totally meshuga. The description would be entirely accurate. I'd had it. Things had piled up from all sides—or, to be fair, I had taken them on—and I was worn out. I had to do something to change that dynamic.

I started to get up. Kane did not release my hands. He was holding them rather tightly.

"Let's get this to go," he said.

"Uh-uh. I'm going to tell them we're on to them."

"You can't."

"I won't say anything more than that, just that they can expect to be hearing from John Law."

"You *can't*," he repeated.

Something about his manner had changed. He was no longer the affable guy who had helped shepherd me through a tough couple of days.

"Why?" I asked.

"Please sit," he said.

I did. But I already knew what he was going to tell me. At least, I had a strong, strong feeling in the *kishkes*.

"You planted the receipt," I said.

He seemed a little taken aback but not insulted. He lowered his eyes.

I sat hard. Everything, not just the anger, seemed to seep out of me and sag over the edge of the seat. Our food arrived. I looked at Kane through the steam.

"Are you going to explain?" I asked.

"I don't think I should."

"That's not what I asked," I said. "But a more important question first. Did you put a cell phone in the room too?"

"No," he said. "We were going to find that somewhere else."

"So the phone receipt, obviously, is yours."

He nodded limply. Captain Health had met his kryptonite for the first time and didn't know how to handle it.

"What were you trying to do, impress me?" I asked.

"Partly that," he said. "But partly also—I don't know if I can tell you."

"Try. No, do more than try," I insisted. "Spit it out. I have to know."

Kane looked up hopefully. He must have thought he heard something compassionate in my voice but he was wrong. He obviously didn't find anything helpful in my eyes because after a moment he looked back down again.

"I don't want to talk about it," he said. "I can't."

"Captain Health, powerless in the face of truth."

"No," he said. "In the face of exposure. There's a reason he wears a mask and a costume."

"Spare me the pop psychology. Not in the mood."

"Gwen, I—"

"Stop." I wasn't interested in mea culpas and humility. "How did you hope to pull this off?" I asked. "Ultimately, the evidence wouldn't have supported a legal case, would it? The police would have discovered that the phone you planted didn't call the number that triggered the explosion."

"They would have discovered that I bought the phone so there'd be a number kids could call to get a message to Captain Health," he said.

"And an anonymous caller would have assumed that random purchase was used to detonate a phone bomb . . . why?"

"A store clerk trying to do his or her part? A doctor or nurse who thinks I'm giving false hope to kids? A frustrated banker looking to get some press for the job he really loves? A super villain?"

It was too soon for him to make jokes; at least, I hoped it was a joke. I felt ill.

I motioned the waiter over, asked him to wrap

up my dinner to go. I reached into my bag and found a twenty.

"Let me," he said, taking out his wallet.

"Go to hell," I replied.

"I'm sorry," he said. "They hurt you. I wanted to hurt them."

"Mister, did you get that bass ackward," I said.

"Not the motives—"

"Are you insane or just moronically provincial?" I said with admitted bitterness. "Trust is goal number one. Without that, in any undertaking, you've got nothing. You, Captain Shlemiel, have nothing."

"Fine. You don't have to be insulting."

"Oh, now you're the wounded half? Jesus."

I threw down the twenty, grabbed my sack of food on the way out, and left without looking back at anyone. It was surprisingly easy. I had no feeling inside, bupkes, not even a sense of betrayal. What Kane had done was stupid, my having had any interest in him was stupid and impulsive, and my plan going forward was to forget the whole damn thing—the investigation, Newt collaborating with the enemy, the enemies themselves, and everything else that was presently in my head. Remarkably, I didn't blame myself for anything that I had done over the last two days. It was post-traumatic stress, I told myself. No one would have been thinking clearly.

I walked the long walk until I reached my car and I drove until I reached my home. I had been praying quietly that Kane hadn't gone to his van to catch up to me there. He hadn't. I fed my two cats, microwaved dinner, and flopped on my crappy sofa with the Styrofoam container and chopsticks.

That was when I saw it: a note on the floor. It must have been slipped under the front door and made its way half under the carpet. I went over and picked up the envelope, saw my name handwritten in block letters, and went back to the chair.

"Fan mail from some flounder?" I wondered.

It seemed an appropriate response. If my life wasn't currently a Rocky and Bullwinkle cartoon, I don't know what it was.

I opened the letter with a finger, figuring that if someone were trying to poison me there were easier ways to go about it. It was handwritten in pencil, one side of a large page. The heading at top said Edenist Party in red ink, from a rubber stamp. The spelling was accurate and the thoughts concise:

Dear Miss Gwen Katz:

The police have been to my home asking about fertilizer. I assume they are concerned because it can be used to make a bomb. I want to assure you I was not involved in the attack on your deli and would not even know how to manufacture an explosive. I told them I did not believe in my heart that any of the candidates were responsible. What I did not tell them was that someone recently purchased a large supply

> *of fertilizer from me. Before I mention such a
> thing, I was wondering if I could ride over or if
> you might stop by tomorrow?*
>
> > *Sincerely,*
> > *Moss Post*

"I wonder," I said to the cats, "how you guys would take to having a horse parked in the driveway."

I decided not to find out. I had nothing on the calendar and a trip to his place might be a nice change. And who knows? Maybe the whole antitechnology lifestyle would appeal to me. I once went to the Amish country in Pennsylvania and wondered what it would be like effectively living in the nineteenth century. I looked up his address. He was located on Ashland City Highway facing the Cumberland River. It would be a short drive just west of the city, a little over twenty miles and a half hour . . . longer than that on horseback.

I channel surfed for a bit, checked e-mails, fell asleep in the bathtub, then went to bed for real.

If I had any dreams, I remembered none of them.

Which was the appropriate metaphor to end the day.

Chapter 16

There are all kinds of beautiful. And this morning, when my psyche was all achy, was the perfect time to be reminded of that.

When I lived in the city, a beautiful sight was the sun setting behind the Statue of Liberty or snow blowing down a gray, deserted Fifth Avenue or dark, angry skies behind the United Nations Building, which always seemed apt.

Here, the beauty is pretty much of a piece: virgin hills and timeless waterways. I didn't know how much of that was due to the fact that it didn't pay to develop the area or the owners were from old families for whom the land meant more than money. That was an odd reality for me down here. Things like that mattered. It wasn't just the financial woman who responded to that unfamiliar reality. Jews, who had historically been on the run from oppressors, rarely owned much more than could fit in an ox cart or valise. Land? I couldn't recall the last Katz who owned any until Uncle Murray moved down here and bought the house and deli.

And we know how that turned out.

The other thing that happens down here, relative to this beauty thing, is that as you go from area to area the scents change. It's not like in New York, where hot tar gives way to a peanut vendor, which gives way to truck fumes, which succumb to Hefty bags of trash. Here, if you drive with your window open, the odors go from a kind of neutral smell in the unpolluted city to what was for me one unidentifiable tree or plant smell to another. Occasionally, you got a whiff of dead wildlife or skunk, but they passed quickly.

Post dwelt on a bluff overlooking the slate blue river. Only the flat slate roof of the main house was visible from the road, though I could see at least two other cabins scattered around a couple of acres of farmland. The only crop I could identify was corn. Everything else looked like wheat to me, whether it was or wasn't. Beyond the farmland were groves of various fruit trees running down the gentle slope of the cliff. I assumed they helped prevent erosion; I remembered that much from high school. The stables and compost area were just behind the short, sloping gravel driveway.

The entire compound looked to me as if the original woodland had been pushed back, everything else dropped in however many scores of years before, and then the surrounding trees allowed to spring back. It was a careful, respectfully constructed homestead.

A pair of barking German shepherds announced me from the bottom of the driveway. Three cars were parked there; not everyone who came to work for or with Moss would necessarily ride a horse. I waited on the gravel drive until someone came out to take charge of the dogs. Foreign smells assaulted me. No, not exactly foreign; it was like my cats' litter box writ large. But I didn't have too much time to consider the multiple sources. Moss himself came to quiet the pooches.

A Lincolnesque figure in coveralls emerged from the house and ordered the dogs away. They quieted and ran off. I got out, heard horses whinnying, stalks blowing, smelled the compost, felt like I was in Amish country. The bearded man smiled through spiky gray whiskers, raised his hand in greeting, and walked forward.

"Hark the heralds," he said.

"Shouldn't that be 'bark'?" I asked.

He laughed. "Lord, you are right!"

I offered a hand and he enveloped it in his two huge canvas-skinned paws. He fixed a pair of clear brown eyes on me, framed by deep-crevassed skin. It was protected from the sun by a big, floppy leather hat that sat on gray hair pulled into a long ponytail. It was held in place with what looked like a beaded Native American clasp.

"I know what you're thinkin'," he said.

"What's that?"

"How can a guy so photogenic fail to capture city hall?"

"Photogenic is relative," I pointed out.

"You mean, like President Taft weighing three hundred and forty pounds in just his moustache."

"No, I was thinking of various cultures around the nation, around the world, where tattoos and piercings that were once considered extreme are becoming normal," I said. "And I hope that what someone looks like isn't the only thing people vote for."

"True, true," he said. "There've been some movie star–lookin' folks who've gone down the chute when they opened their mouths."

"Exactly."

I was starting to *shvitz* standing out there and Moss took my arm and walked me toward the small patio surrounded by hanging plants and hardworking bees.

"They won't sting," he assured me as he offered me a lounge in the shade. "Like everyone and everything else around here, they come to work."

"By choice," I said, "which makes it even nicer."

"That's true," he said. "Our team of farmers and election workers and even our livestock are committed."

I smiled and sat. He lowered himself into a wooden chair. It was funny. I'd been around so many older Jewish men all my life, I'd expected him to say "Oy" as he sat. He pulled the chair closer. I think he did that as a little show of intimacy, not security. There was no one outside of this household for miles around.

"Would you like anything?" he asked. "Fresh milk?"

"Had my cuppa joe en route, thanks," I said.

"Ah, coffee. I gave it up years ago for tea. I once thought of growing my own beans here but coffee can be a stubborn crop, I'm told."

"Must be all that caffeine."

He grinned. "What about a tour? You might find it a little different from what you're accustomed to. You don't look like you get out to farms much."

"I look like I don't? Why?"

He pointed toward my feet. "City soles. Out here you need something that'll go an inch or two into muck."

"I do not own such a pair," I admitted. "If it's okay with you, all I'd like is to know why you sent me that note."

"I asked one of my campaign workers to drop it at your place because I felt you should know."

"Yes, but why not the police?"

"Because anything I say or do is going to be declared 'political,'" he said. "I don't work that way. I wanted you to know I am a man of integrity. It's important."

"I see." I did respect his intentions, which I took to be sincere. Rare, a little odd, but earnest.

"I am also not implying anything, only presenting the facts," he said.

"Okay," I said. "So—the person in question?"

"I sold eight bags to Josephine Young," he told me.

"Owner of the Salad Barre," I said, not terribly surprised. "That Josephine Young?"

"That's right."

"New client?"

"Uh huh. She said she believed that several of her organic providers were not providing true organics and intended to start farming her own. I recall there was a competition in which you beat her for some prize—"

"Best Mid-range Restaurant," I said.

"That's it. I know that she is a competitive lady, that she came from a highly competitive art, and—honestly, I have no reason to doubt her but I also don't know how far she would go to win this year."

It's funny. Not ha-ha funny but sick funny. I didn't believe someone would kill to become mayor of Nashville. But I wouldn't put it past someone who put their heart into a business to go to extremes to make that business a success.

"Was there anything strange or furtive about the way she bought the fertilizer?" I asked.

"She's a kind of strange duck to begin with, but nothing beyond that."

"Did she come alone?"

"No," he said thoughtfully. "She had a helper. A guy who did the lugging."

"Did you recognize him?"

Moss shook his head. "It could've been someone she knew or who worked for her or someone she hired to help her for an hour."

"Right. What did he look like?" Moss obviously didn't talk to a lot of people, either. Getting information from him was like getting eggs from gefilte fish.

"Hunky guy, bald, late thirties, I'd say. Rough hands, rough shaven, probably blue collar."

"Barrel chested, on the stumpy side?"

"Yeah, yeah—"

"Sounds like Gar McQueen," I said. "He's a lawn-care guy, does a lot of work for downtown businesses."

"It's very possible he's the man. He had the look."

"Did he say anything?"

"Grunted a lot, but I don't blame him. Those bags were heavier than dry cement." Moss laughed. He pronounced the word "see-ment." There was something quaint about that. "I give people their money's worth of manure."

He had that in common with other politicians, I thought.

"I'm going to have to think about what to do with this information," I said. "But in any case, I won't tell anyone where I heard it."

"I appreciate that."

There didn't seem to be anything else and, declining a horseback ride which would not have ended well for me or My Friend Flicka, I stood and thanked him.

"If you don't get into town much, what are you going to do if you win the election?" I asked.

"Get in more," he replied with a wink. "I believe in what I stand for, Ms. Katz—limiting cell phone towers and cables and expanded roads and everything that's destroying our local beauty and heritage. That's worth gettin' off my duff for."

Once again, I found him more admirable than impressive, and seriously unlikely to win the election. He seemed to think so too, because apart from a poster stuck to a stake at the front of the driveway, I saw nothing that indicated a campaign was in full swing.

I decided to swing by Josephine's home on the way back. Not to talk to her but to eyeball the place and see if all that fertilizer was actually being used. I got her home address from the Nashville Restaurant Authority website—a members-only organization for the airing of grievances and little else. Like most associations, they certainly didn't solve any problems, mutual or otherwise.

Josephine lived in a small brick house set toward the front of a three-acre lot on Peach Blossom Square. Most of the property was out back, which was where she was doing her gardening. Or rather, that's where Gar was doing it. She was already at her restaurant. The lawn-care professional was in the back planting in the areas of lawn that had been newly torn up and fertilized.

She's certainly doing what she said she'd be doing with the bags, I thought. I tried to count how many were out there but I was at a bad angle. I didn't want to go back there and tip my hand, especially if Josephine had been behind the blast. There was certainly enough fertilizer there to level the block I live on.

I drove on, having learned very little from the morning's adventure—though there was one thing I wondered as I drove away.

What if Josephine wasn't the one who used some of this fertilizer?

I stopped the car, made a U-turn, and went back to Josephine's house.

Chapter 17

I parked curbside and walked around the Josephine Young homestead. There was a forehead-high hedge to my left and a two-yard-wide swath of rich green grass that bumped up against a rose garden beside the house. It smelled very aromatic here, the floral scent trapped in the narrow passage. I understood something about the South, just then. People moved slowly not just because of the heat but because it allowed you to literally stop and smell the roses. Move through it quickly and it would dissipate like mist. You would think something like that would have been obvious. But in a world where everything was rush-rush, the obvious was often buried and overlooked. I didn't bother to count how many layers of my life had to be removed to get me here, to that realization.

I rounded the back of the house where the scent mixed with the decidedly different odor of fertilizer. It wasn't unpleasant; it was just different, like the Moss farm but without the big valley wind to blow the smells away.

Gar was shirtless. He had a bulk that suggested strength but without strong, youthful definition. It wasn't an athletic look, not like the hospital superhero whose name must not be mentioned; it was more like a dockworker.

He looked up as I sauntered around the corner. "Mr. McQueen? I saw your truck out front, saw you working here."

Now, at this point, someone thus addressed would talk back. Say howdy, smile, grunt. I expected him to do one of those, since I potentially represented work, a new client. He didn't. He stopped hoeing long enough to look at me and wait for whatever was coming next. I had nothing, so I fumbled through.

"My name is Gwen Katz and I—"

"I know who you are," he answered. He said it like he'd seen my *punim* on a wanted poster and was giving me sixty seconds to turn my horse's *tuchas* toward him and head out of town.

"Oh," I replied. "Is knowing me a good thing or a bad thing?"

"It's a no-thing," he said.

"Do you mean n-o or k-n-o-w?"

He didn't answer. The way he had spoken reminded me of a prizefighter who was really good at one thing—beating the *kishkes* out of people, or in this case, planting stuff—and then went still and dumb when he wasn't doing that. For example, trying to speak.

"Anyway, I was wondering if you might have

time to do some work at my home," I went on. "I live on Bonerwood Drive, the least crappy looking place on the block, but I think it can be made to look even less crappy still—"

"Not today," he answered dismissively. "I'm working."

"No, it wouldn't have to be today," I replied.

"I mean, I can't even think about it today," he said. "I'm doing *this*."

"Right," I said. "Of course."

"Call the number on the truck and leave a message," he said. "I'll call back when I have my calendar."

"All right," I said. "Is this a real busy time of year for you?"

He looked annoyed. "I'm always busy. Lawns and gardens are important."

"I know. I just thought there'd be a lot of competition, that people would be eager to have work—"

"That's not an issue for me!" he crowed, and suddenly got very articulate. "Ms. Katz, some people go to school for this. A whole bunch of those people are accountants or teachers who can't get those jobs, or people who became real estate agents until the bottom fell outta that and thought this would be a good alternative. They're too educated or too uneducated. I apprenticed," he said proudly, actually slapping his hairless chest and sending beads of sweat flying. "I know the earth. I get results."

"I understand," I told him truthfully. "And I admire that. Josephine obviously does as well."

"She is an artist. I am an artist."

"I see. You don't mean her restaurant, you mean she was a dance artist—"

"*Is*," he said. "*Is* a dancer. I have seen DVDs."

The gardener glared at me for a moment and then went back to work.

I turned back toward the street. I had learned absolutely nothing about the fertilizer and its possible role in blowing up my deli. But I had learned a little about the man, a loyal man who might be easily manipulated by a strong woman—and by that I mean, sadly, a strong woman other than me. Perhaps he would conceive of doing something to impress her—such as taking out the competitor who had won the restaurant competition.

There was something smelly here, I felt, and it had nothing to do with manure. Some people were antisocial . . . but a businessperson who was unenthusiastic about business? That didn't sit right with this former Wall Streeter. While he was hidden behind the house, I was tempted to have a look inside his truck, see what there was to see. From where I stood, it looked a little messy. Maybe he used the back seat as a place to toss garbage. I did. The address on the side was a post office box which suggested he carried the business around with him . . . possibly on the laptop sitting in the bucket of the passenger's seat. But with enough traffic and daylight on the street, having a look at it here and now, even if he were logged on, didn't seem like the greatest idea.

He looked up as I drove away, our eyes locking for the briefest moment as I passed the other side of the house. I went home and, with a Coke and a smile and my laptop on my lap, I did some Web checking on Gar McQueen. Now you may ask, *Gwen, by your own meshuga reasoning shouldn't every gardener in Nashville be a suspect?*

Theoretically.

But my little ballet dancer restaurant rival had a potential motive, Gar was working with her, and it was at least worth checking to see if the burly landscaper had anything that could conceivably tie him to questionable acts, including hate crimes.

His Facebook page did not have many privacy settings, so I was able to see the usual sports Likes and family stuff. No siblings but a lot of young cousins. Just being there, scrolling through photos of silly people pouting their lips and making rock star gestures, bored me out of my skull. I left the social media, dug into newspaper archives, and found articles going back two years about what he was landscaping and where, and a couple of awards he had won. I even found a photo of him as third runner-up in a bodybuilding competition four years earlier.

Okay, so he wasn't a prizefighter, but he might've dropped some dumbbells on himself. The weight lifting would explain my first impression of his bare-chested body. He looked pretty good in the photo, greased up in his little trunks. He must have given up competition after that since he didn't look quite as buff these days. That used to be a debate around the dinner table in the Katz home. Not about bodybuilding but about giving up. My mother used to think it was negligent and irresponsible to give up on anything until the job was done or the goal achieved. My father, predictably—given his history in the area of *farlozn*, quitting—thought it was the wise man or woman who knew when to retreat and try something else. Me, being like a dog with a bone in all things, naturally sided with my mother.

I considered the photo a moment longer. Gar had lost just like Josephine had lost. Maybe he identified with her, imagined her disappointment, looked to settle the score on behalf of a woman he admired.

Putting the puzzle aside for the moment, I checked on my hospital-bound staff. Thom was awake but groggy from her medication, A.J. was still critical but somewhat responsive, and the nurses I spoke with seemed guardedly optimistic with the "you-didn't-hear-this-from-me-Ms.-Katz" caveats. I decided not to visit. It might sound strange but I felt a little toxic. It wasn't as if I'd done anything wrong or could have prevented this thing from happening. But with the live-or-die threat gone, I worried that A.J. Two or someone else might see me and suddenly think, "Hey—we want our pound of flesh." If that were going to happen, I didn't want to see it dawn in their eyes.

I called my attorney and insurance agent in turn. As yet, my attorney hadn't received any notifications about complaints from the staff, but that was still my biggest fear. It wasn't just the idea that my employees, my friends, my de facto family could become adversaries, it was also the prolonged aggravation and expense of such an action. My attorney reminded me that while a few days had passed, that didn't mean we were out of the woods, not at all. Luke, A.J. Two, Dani, and others, including Benjamin and Grace, might still be weighing the pros and cons of such an action.

Which made finding out who did it even more imperative. Let someone else's insurance agency knock themselves out worrying about this.

Speaking of insurance, my brief chat with agent Zebeck was surprisingly succinct. He was wading through the miasma of electronic filing and bureaucracy and had only one question for me.

"Do you want to rebuild or abandon?" he asked.

"Just like that?" I asked, a little surprised.

"It's a big, basic question that needs to be answered."

"*To be or not to be . . .* ," I thought. I'd gone from Shylock to Hamlet without leaving my sofa. "Good God, Alan, I don't know. We don't even know how long it would take to reboot the place."

"That's right, and I can't ask for an evaluation and cost estimate until you've weighed in," he said.

"When do I have to let you know?"

"I wouldn't take more than another day or

so," he said. "Whatever you decide would send things in a different direction in terms of what we file and with whom. There are not only insurance considerations but city deadlines as well."

"Understood. I'll let you know sometime tomorrow."

I surprised myself by my indecision. I thought I would have told him to put Humpty Dumpty back together, bigger and better than ever. Was I that afraid to face my people or was I really and truly beaten by a place where I probably didn't belong, by people with whom I didn't have a whole lot in common, by men who were less venal but more disturbingly clueless than the putzes I'd left behind in Manhattan? Whatever the case, I had just given myself twenty-four hours to figure it all out.

Those chores done—and they were all onerous, something I hadn't realized until I was done and felt a whole lot lighter—I phoned Detective Bean. The good inspector said they were still reviewing forensics and security cameras, still conducting interviews, and she had nothing to report.

"Nothing to report or nothing to report to me?" I pressed.

"The latter," she admitted. "Have you looked at the newspapers or their websites?"

I admitted I had not.

"The papers are reporting that it was not a gas explosion, which is accurate," she said. "Sources tell the press that the bomb was planted, which is accurate."

"Homemade?"

"Apparently, since dynamite or plastic explosives would have left a crater where the deli is standing and identifiable chemical traces," the detective said. "Candy Sommerton is reporting that the Metro Police are considering several persons of interest, which is true if a bit strong. We're doing a thorough by-the-book investigation."

Ah, Candy. Saying the same thing with a different slant creates news where there isn't any.

"Candy also reported that this was not a politically motivated act, which may be accurate. None of the candidates seem to have that level of animus for one another."

"Their aides?"

"Checking that," the detective admitted. "Eager beavers are always a possibility and a problem."

"And me?" I asked. "Does anyone you've talked to have that level of animus toward me?"

"You have not been offered police protection," she pointed out.

That was an answer, at least by inference. It suggested that the police didn't think I was the target. That was something of a relief, given my paranoia and my track record.

"What about the butcher?" I asked. "Could the bomb have been in his container and meant to go off earlier or meant for his daughter while she was making deliveries?"

"We've talked to all the protestors who were at

his shop, run checks, found nothing other than unpaid parking tickets and domestic disturbance arrests. As for Alex and Sandy Potts, he seems to adore his daughter and she does not appear to be suicidal."

That would have been my reading as well. The idea that Alex would attempt to kill her or that she would attempt to kill herself and take others with her was a chilling thought. That didn't make it impossible, but it went onto the backmost of my back burners.

"Can I ask one more thing?" I said.

"Go ahead. And Ms. Katz—you do know I'm not trying to be evasive here."

"I know that, Detective. I appreciate everything you're doing for me. I'm not used to compassion in authority figures."

She actually chuckled at that. "Believe it or not, this helps me too."

"How so?"

"Reminds me that there are people, like me, at the other end of these situations. What was that last question you had?"

Her openness had gotten me off track. I hopped back on. "Right. Has Homeland Security gotten involved?"

"TOHS is automatically informed about incidents of this type," Bean said, referring to the Tennessee Office of Homeland Security. "All relevant data is being sent there. So far, they have not sent anything back with a red flag."

"So this is really a big bag of bupkes."

"If I understand the word correctly—"

"It means bird poop," I said. "Just a bit. Not a real bad curse."

"Charming," Bean replied.

"It kind of is," I explained.

"Then you believe there's been little progress."

"I believe there is little to go on, thus impeding progress," I told her. I didn't want her to think I was running her efforts down. Or bird pooping on them.

"I don't agree," she replied. "Often, the elimination of major suspects and motives is more progress than following a tiny thread. That is the phase we are in now. What's left when that process is completed will give us a much more manageable situation. I guess you could say we're clearing away the bupkes one pigeon at a time."

"Sorry," I said. "I didn't mean to impugn what you are doing."

"I know what you meant," Bean replied. "And frankly, we're frustrated too. We're either dealing with an amateur or a professional who made the crime scene look like the work of an amateur."

"That sounds sinister."

"If it's true, yes."

We chatted a little more in generalities, about how background checks on the "new people" in the hole—Benjamin and Grace—hadn't brought up anything similar, and we parted no more or less friendly than when we started. For me, that was something of a novelty.

The procedural aspect of the case aside, going from big to small was her way of saying that the trail was not so much cold as the evidence really, really thin. What *that* told me was there were no uniquely specialized ingredients in the bomb. Otherwise, they'd have a direction in which to move.

And at least the lady took my call. She didn't have to do that. Grant used to, of course, but then he was a detective with benefits and I was a stationary target at times. Bean truly seemed to want to be of assistance. Maybe it was girl-bonding or professionalism or both. Whatever the reason, I was grateful for it.

What all of this information did to me, of course, was the antithesis of everything that good lady stood for. It made me want to chuck all the due process, ignore technicalities like search warrants, chuck all the other legal *shmontses*, and get some answers. I knew myself well enough to understand that the answer Alan Zebeck had asked for would not come until this thing had been settled.

And so I took a nap, resolved to get some answers whenever my brain poked me awake.

Chapter 18

I was awakened by the classic bing-bong of the doorbell.

I had been in a happy dream place, with ducks on a pond—something I had experienced once in my life, when I was six or seven years old and my parents went to visit a friend in Norwalk, Connecticut. I remember the fearlessness of those real-life ducks while I threw them Oysterette crackers. My father kept saying "Oy" with each throw. I didn't get the joke then, and it wasn't in my dream. The ducks in my head were all stuck in the pond and quacking their displeasure. I tried to calm them and couldn't, couldn't find the Oysterettes, started to get agitated myself.

And then the doorbell.

It was three-fifteen on the DVR clock across from the sofa. I hoped it wasn't Captain Health, all repentant and apologetic.

"Coming!" I said as I threw off the throw I'd pulled over me. I stumbled to the door, stuck in that clinging nap-sleep. I widened my eyes to wake myself, ran my fingers through my hair, and pulled the door open.

Two of my little duckies stood there on the front stoop. I switched on the front light and Luke and Dani looked up at me with what I would best describe as ashamed little smiles. To continue my animal metaphor, they were like cats who seemed pleased to have eaten the goldfish even though they knew they shouldn't have.

"Hey," they both said, using the word that had mysteriously supplanted the traditional "Hi" in everyone's lexicon.

"Shalom," I replied, still a little groggy. "Come in."

They looked at me a little mystified, then at each other, and then they giggled. I stepped back to admit them. Even as they walked in, Luke was pulling something from the back pocket of his jeans. I experienced a jolt as I realized it could be some kind of legal letter. Grinning, he handed it to me. I opened it as I knocked the door shut with my knee.

It wasn't from an attorney. It was from the city.

It was a marriage license. I smiled as I took it in, grinned as I saw their names on it, felt a little guilty when I thought that with nothing else to do they'd decided to get married, then looked up at them. They were standing like punk figures on a cake, thin and innocent despite the tattoos and piercings, Dani's little fingers wrapped in Luke's larger ones, the picture of young love drawn by an artist for Adult Swim.

"I am so happy for you both." I beamed. And I was.

Dani tittered. "Being, like, so near death made us realize how we wanted to die together, whenever that might be."

I resisted saying, "*And getting married* will *guarantee your death . . .*" Instead, I said, "Well . . . that's a big and very adult step."

"True." Luke nodded. "But, like, we're already living together so stuff won't cost any more."

"I think there's a saying, right?" Dani asked.

"Two can live as cheaply as one," I offered.

"That's it!"

Luke went on, "Plus the lawyer said we'll have some money from the accident so that will help us as we figure out what to do."

My spine went icy and stiff. "The lawyer?"

"That man," Dani said.

"The one who has been to the deli," Luke added.

"Dickson?" I asked.

"Yes, Dickson Three, like A.J. Two," Dani giggled.

Andrew A. Dickson III, I thought. So, there will be a claim.

The two kids standing in front of me were giddy from what they had done today, not what they were telling me. I'm not sure they even really understood. But they weren't *shmeckle;* they needed to know.

"You do realize that he's talking about suing me," I said.

They stopped laughing slowly, like my dream

ducks paddling from shore and being swallowed by mist.

"What are you talking about?" Luke asked.

"Yah . . . he said there was a class of some kind," Dani said. "We'd take it with an insurance company."

"A class action suit," I said. "He represents a bunch of you, he sues me and the deli in court, and the insurance company has to pay all of you if the judge or jury thinks I was somehow negligent."

"Whoa, wait," Luke said. "What are you talking about? Who said anything about suing you?"

"Luke, what the hell did you think the attorney was planning?"

"Just what Dani said," he replied with a puzzled expression. He looked at her and she nodded up in perplexed agreement.

"I think you'd better have him explain this slowly and carefully before you agree to anything," I said. "Did you sign anything?"

"Just some papers saying it was okay with us for him to, like, do his lawyer thing," Luke told me.

"Who else?" I asked. "Besides you two, who else signed with him?"

"Raylene, A.J. Two, and Newt," he said.

"I think Thom said no," Dani remarked. It was as if Dani were one of those ducks, peering through the mist, trying to make out the opposite shore. "He said something about her—what was the word he used? Option?"

"Opting?" I asked. "Opting out?"

Dani snapped her painted fingertips and pointed. "That's it."

"Gwen, I'm not really liking this vibe," Luke said. "Are you saying that we did something wrong?"

"Wrong?" I asked. "Legally, no. You're within your rights to sue me and the deli. Morally? You guys know I had nothing to do with what happened and couldn't have prevented it. Claims like this are opportunistic and attorneys like Dickson are known as ambulance chasers." I saw Dani trying to keep up. "It means they see an accident and rush over, get the victim to sign papers like you signed. When the insurance company pays up—and most times they do—the attorney keeps a third or more of the money."

"Nice racket," Luke said.

"That's exactly what it is," I said. "A legal racket."

"But the money doesn't come from you," Dani said, clearly wanting to clarify. "It comes from a company."

"At first it does," I said. "See, I pay a yearly premium to my insurance company to cover me from accidents or situations like this. When they have to pay out any big settlement, the yearly premiums of *all* of their clients go up. That way, the insurance company still makes a profit."

"Huh," Luke said. "Like I heard you say when coffee bean prices went up. You had a big new weekly expense so, like, you raised the price on everybody's cup a little bit to cover your cost."

"Exactly," I said, impressed that he made the connection.

"But you're also saying it won't cost you very much and that everyone in the class can get a lot of money," Dani said.

"Actually, my premium will go up considerably because insurance also has to pay to rebuild . . . if I rebuild," I added.

"Hmmm," Luke said.

It wasn't that Luke and Dani were stupid. They were not. They were, like so many of their generation, simply focused on the minutiae of whatever they needed to know—like music or jewelry or how their latest tech gadget worked— and let the Internet tell them everything else.

"So does this make us, like, enemies?" Dani asked.

I took a long, long moment to think before answering. I didn't want to encourage Dani or Luke into thinking that this kind of opportunistic shakedown was okay. But I also didn't want to have them run back to Dickson and say that I threatened or antagonized them. All I needed was for him to get in front of a judge and say that I tried to cow or coerce my employees. That could also open the door to labor issues, a door I had no doubt that *shmendrick* would love to kick open.

"You work for me but we have become friends," I said, "and we must always remain friends. That is more important than any other consideration. At least, it is to me."

The two young people looked down, at each

other, down again, made faces that suggested they were processing what I had said. All the while they held hands. I realized I was still holding the marriage license. I looked back at it.

"This is major," I said with a chuckle. "I'm so happy for you both. Are you going to have a wedding? You know, a gown and bridesmaids, thrown rice, all of that?"

"We want to have it at one of the clubs where Luke plays," Dani said, her mind still clearly struggling with the previous subject. "Nothing fancy. Just a bunch of friends, a little bit of family, and a lot of fun."

"Sounds perfect," I said.

"Yeah," Luke replied.

"Hey, I hope your band doesn't expect to get paid," Dani said, playing with the zipper on his hoodie. "Like, they're guests but they still have to play so you can serenade us and stuff."

"Yeah," Luke agreed. "I'll talk to them."

Then they fell awkwardly silent. I let it stay like that for a bit, then asked, "What's up?"

Luke's mouth moved around a little, testing it like the Tin Man after he'd been oiled. He didn't speak.

"We, uh—we, like, are planning to pay for stuff with the money Dickson said he's going to get us," Dani said. "Except for the band, who better play for free."

"We can't afford stuff otherwise," Luke said.

"Like clothes to get married in," Dani added. "And food."

The silence returned, thicker and more uncomfortable than before. I think if they could have clicked their heels to vanish—to continue the allusion—they would have done so. What was sad was that I would have offered to pay for the wedding as my gift to them, but Dickson would have turned that into coercion.

I handed Luke the license. "Listen," I said, "I am really happy for you both, and I don't want a good day to go bad for you. Go wherever you were going, have a great little celebration, and don't worry about anything."

"But we have to," Luke said. "We don't want to hurt you."

"You won't," I assured them. I didn't know if they could tell I was lying. Luke and I had worked together every day since I arrived in Nashville. Often, our nonverbal signals were more useful than what we said. From the way he was looking at me, his head slightly bowed but his eyes on me, he might be doing that now.

Dani hugged me and thanked me and Luke smiled thinly as he turned to leave. Something got through to them, though I don't know exactly what that was. It truly had not been my intention to manipulate them in any way. Did I want Andrew Dickson III to go away, or worse? Yes. Did I want to cause Luke and Dani concern? No. Especially not on a day that was so important to them.

They both gave me little waist-high waves as they left. I shut the door and exhaled. That was tougher than I thought; the punch from being told that Dickson was, in fact, coming after me was hard and ugly. I was glad to feel anger at him, though, and not at my two workers, though it bothered me a little that Raylene, A.J. Two, and Newt—the little traitor, of all people—had jumped on for the trip to Fort Knox. But it also touched me to learn that Thom had not. Say whatever bad things you want about organized religion, it gave her a moral compass and the backbone to reject things she felt were wrong. Then again, Dickson had screwed over her brother in a property dispute and Thom actually went to jail for a few hours after the lawyer provoked her into coming after him with a Windex bottle. So I knew she would never be involved with any situation in which he would benefit.

Eating a toasted bagel with *shmear* as a late afternoon snack while I got my digital camera and whatever else I thought I'd need, I dressed for my little excursion. Then, filled with bitter indignation at Dickson—which got stacked on the anger I already felt for whoever did this—I headed out.

Chapter 19

According to the online white pages, my quarry lived in a very small house on Lucile Street. The ride took twenty minutes. As I made the turn off N. First Street, I saw a quaint little shoebox house with what seemed to be a lush lawn and ample garden, all of it behind a very high chain-link fence. I worried that the fence meant there might be a dog, in which case this would be a very short drive-by. But I didn't see any areas of the lawn or garden that were dug up. Judging from the weedy, burnt lawns of the houses that surrounded his, I guessed that Gar simply didn't want dogs or kids or ATVs or guilty husbands looking for a rose ripping up what he had so carefully planted.

I pulled to the curb across the street, and sat there idling. Gar's truck was in the driveway, which was behind the fence. If I were going to get to it and have a snoop, I was going to have to climb. I hadn't done *that* since I was a kid. I had smaller feet then, which fit easily in the openings. Now, I wasn't so sure.

Worth it? I asked myself as I sat burning gas at four bucks a gallon.

I wasn't sure what I was going to do at the truck, other than look inside and hope he wouldn't see me from the house. I didn't think it would be smart to open the truck door and, besides, he probably took the laptop inside. Still, my gut told me to do it; I figured I'd know whatever I was looking for when I found it— maybe a wrapper from deli takeout, a cryptic note from Josephine, another ingredient used to make a bomb. Something.

Or nothing, I told myself. Maybe I just wanted to cross him and Josephine off the list.

Or maybe I just wanted to be proactive.

"That's it, isn't it?" I asked myself quietly. I couldn't do anything about Dickson or poor Thom or A.J. I couldn't go to work. I didn't want to talk to Captain Health. I felt like I had nothing and no one and was trying to throw a little confetti in the air, cheer myself up. Back in New York, I used to do that by going to the movies or a concert or meeting a friend for brunch. Now, I was out prowling. I was the Catwoman.

Or Katzwoman.

Oy, I thought. A superhero reference. *Stop it; that's Iger's shtick.*

My brain really was going a little stir crazy.

I sat there because I really didn't have a plan of action and I also didn't have anywhere else to go, no one to see. Why did Iger have to turn out to be such a putz? Maybe it was time for a dating site.

I was about to drive away when I saw something move from the corner of my eye. I turned as Gar came out the front door, wearing his overalls and a fawn-colored windbreaker. I snapped off the engine, watched as the landscaper went to the gate, opened it, then pulled the truck out. He got out and closed the gate. I fired up my lazy six-cylinder and followed as he drove off.

He headed south, back the way I had come. It was actually a little scary as I realized he could be heading directly for my house. It was late to be paying a professional call, and he hadn't been dressed for a date. He bypassed the city center, which is where he might find a hoedown kind of bar. This was the route to Bonerwood Drive and I was starting to get really concerned. Not that I was in any danger, since I was stealthily traveling behind him. I was worried that my paranoia was dead-on. If he was heading to my house, he might have it in mind to blow that up too. With me in it.

My heart was punching my rib cage on three sides. Dammit, he *was* going to my place. I let myself fall back a few more car lengths. The road was going to get pretty deserted up ahead on Edmondson and I didn't want him to see me. I needed to know what the lawn mower man was up to.

Now my palms were *shvitzing* all over the steering wheel. Sweat was dribbling down my shirt collar. Without taking my eyes from the road, I fished around my bag and retrieved my cell phone. I dropped it on the seat where it would be handy. I had Detective Bean's number saved and would call her at once if he stopped at Casa Katz.

We drove down Edmondson. There was no doubt now. He slowed, made the turn onto Bonerwood. I stopped down the street as though I lived somewhere else. I picked up the phone and watched while he checked the numbers, stopped in front of my place. He did not get out of the truck. He looked the place over, just like I'd done with his. And it was pretty clear with no car in the driveway and dusk setting in with no lights on inside that no one was home.

I picked up the phone and punched it on—

As he looked over at my car, I slumped low in the seat. He turned the truck around and drove toward me. Maybe he'd just drive by and go—

But he pulled up next to me, driver's side to driver's side. He was higher than me and looked down with the face of a judge about to pass sentence.

"I figured it was you," he said.

"Oh? Why?"

"I saw your car as you drove past Josephine's house," he said. "I thought I saw it on the way down."

"Well, you did," I said stupidly.

"You got my message?" he asked.

"Uh . . . no. I did not."

I looked at my phone. There was a voice-mail message from Gar McQueen.

"Josephine gave me your number," he said. "I figured you were maybe too busy to call so I decided I'd come around and have a look at the place. You did say this is where you wanted work done?"

"Yes. I did. That's right." I felt like the world's number one shmuck.

Gar looked back at the house as if measuring the distance with his eyes. "So—why did you park about an eighth of a mile away?"

"I . . . I didn't know it was you up there," I said, stumbling. "I just saw someone pull up in front of my place, got concerned. I'm a little cautious since the bombing."

He nodded. "Understandable. So you didn't see the big lawn mower in the back and the name on the side?"

"Couldn't make out either of them," I told him lamely. "Not the best eyes in the world."

He looked down at me wearing the same flat expression he'd had on back at Josephine's. "So you want to talk about your place?"

I sighed a big, trembling sigh. "I'm sort of bushed. No pun intended. But, I mean, you're here already if you want to look around."

He was still looking back. "Sure."

That was all he said. He swung the truck around and went back to the house. I felt a little better having spoken to him, pretty sure now that he hadn't come to put a bomb in the trash can or something. But then, I couldn't be sure that he wouldn't either.

He drove back, I followed, and, while I pulled into the driveway, he walked around, though it was really starting to get dark.

"You got a patio light?" he asked.

"Blown out," I said. Which is why it wasn't on. I was always in a rush in the morning and usually got home when it was dark, not the easiest way to change a light bulb that required a step stool.

"Get a bulb," he said. "I'll do it for you."

"You really don't—"

"It'll help me see," was all he said.

I said okay, went inside, and got the stool and bulb. The joke of this all, of course, was that I really didn't want anything done on the lawn. Not unless I was going to sell the place, a thought that was starting to *noodge* me in the back of my brain. It took all of a minute and there was light.

He hopped down and looked around. "Boy," was all he said.

"I know. I never had a lawn in New York."

"You city people," he said. "Did you have a car?"

"No—"

"But you got one of those. Lawns, your home, should be just as important. It makes a statement about our pride as a homeowner, improves our mood with its beauty and aroma. This is depressing."

I was beginning to think the guy was sincere. I was guessing—call it a crazy Gwen Katz hunch—that mad bombers didn't talk so passionately about foliage.

He walked around, felt the soil, pulled up some clumps, brushed off his hands, shook his head, and paced the grounds like a prisoner on his exercise break, part shuffle, part introspection. After about five minutes he came back.

"It'll cost a lot to do what I have in mind, what I think needs to be done," he said.

"Blow everything up?" I asked.

He looked at me strangely. "Boy, you have an odd sense of vocabulary."

That was an odd statement, but I understood it. "Yes, my outlook is a little weird."

"To finish what I was saying, every square inch of this yard needs to be turned over by hand," he said. "You may need a lot of new soil since this stuff is dry and depleted. Not surprising since there hasn't been a lot of rotting foliage out here to nourish it. Plus I'd have to build some areas up to control the runoff when you water and when it rains. There's also going to be good quality seed and that's just the basics. I'd recommend a garden, some hedges, maybe even a little fountain to add a touch of elegance, a centerpiece. Anyway, I can work something up if you're serious. Take some photos when the light is better so I can show you what things will look like."

"And give me a price," I added.

"Of course."

That would be my out. I'd feel a little guilty making him do all that work, but I really couldn't afford it with the deli down . . . though it wasn't the worst idea in the world. Even if I decided to put Nashville in my rearview mirror, I'd still need to "doll things up," as my aunt Rose used to say.

Feeling silly for my concerns, I walked Gar to his truck. He hadn't loosened up much but, as he'd said, he was an artist. He took this stuff seriously.

"Thanks for taking the initiative on this," I said. "Sorry I didn't call."

"I'm sure you've been preoccupied," he said.

"Not with anything I've really wanted to do."

"Except to come and talk with me about landscaping."

"Yeah," I said.

He regarded me before he got into the truck. "How did you happen to know where I was this morning?"

The question caught me flat-footed. "Oh. I just figured you'd be at Josephine's place."

"Why? She's not my only client."

"Someone mentioned you were doing work for her," I said. "As a matter of fact it may have been Josephine—I was at her restaurant."

"Hmmm," he hummed.

"Hmmm what?"

"That's not very likely. She doesn't enjoy sharing."

"Well, then it must have been someone else," I said.

"It must have been," he said.

"You sound suspicious."

"No. Just a little bit puzzled." He smirked and got into the truck. I don't think he knew it was Moss—how could he?—but he knew I was lying. If he cared, he didn't let on. "By the way," he said as he fired up his engine, "while I was looking back at your car, I could've sworn I saw somebody tailing *you*."

The base of my spine felt little electric eels writhing around. "Seriously?"

"Why would I lie to you?" he asked.

He pointed. I looked back just as a car, its lights off, was turning and leaving Bonerwood Drive.

"You don't suppose it could have been Josephine?" I asked.

He actually honked out a little laugh at that.

"Why is that funny?" I asked. "You said she's possessive."

"Yeah, but I didn't say she's crazy like that lady from the cartoon, the one who wanted to turn dogs into coats!"

It took me a moment. "You mean Cruella De Vil? From *101 Dalmatians*?"

"I don't know. I saw it with my daughter when she was little."

"You have a daughter?" I asked ridiculously—because he had just said so.

"I do," he told me. "She's fourteen now and lives with her mother in Birmingham, Alabama."

Ordinarily I would have asked a follow-up question because it was the first really personal, human thing the man had said to me. But my eyes were still on Edmondson and my mind and lower back were still preoccupied with the idea that some unknown third party may have been out there watching me for reasons unknown.

"I'll let you know about the lawn in a few days," Gar said.

I shot him a look that bordered on startled. In just a second or two, I'd forgotten he was there.

"Yes—I'd appreciate that. And thanks for coming out. Sorry I was so—I don't know. Whatever I was."

He gave me another of his slightly critical looks and drove away. I watched him go with a trace of regret. The brake lights threw a blood red color on the street and then it was dark. And quiet. And lonely. I briefly considered driving out again and seeing if I could find whoever may have been watching me—but that didn't seem to make any sense. I had no idea who to look for or which way to go. The joke about this all was that I had set out to trap someone who was probably innocent—and, in so doing, found out that someone else was probably watching me.

I got my stuff from the car, the tools that I was going to employ to become an ace detective, not one of which I had actually used. Feeling stupid on top of everything else, I went back inside. I turned off the outside light—it was nice to have it back—but I didn't bother turning on any inside lights. Instead, I pulled a kitchen chair to the dark window near the front door and sat looking at the street. I couldn't see very far, but I would certainly be able to see if anyone came back.

Now that Gar was gone, they might. If they did, I wanted to see them.

I kept the cell phone on my lap, plugged in so the battery wouldn't *plotz*, Detective Bean's number under my thumb. My heart had slowed, but not by that much. I ignored the cats, who were twining round and round at my feet precisely because they felt ignored. My eyes adjusted to the dark, my ears filtered out the familiar noises of the neighborhood: the occasional dog and airplane, the elderly Camerons next door who sat outside on warmish nights like this, the cars whose music and motors were familiar to me. I wanted whoever had been here to come back. I wanted someone to blame, a focus for the turmoil I felt.

At some point I fell asleep. I woke shortly after ten p.m. according to that device-of-all-trades, the DVR, and as my eyes came to life, I looked outside and saw something that brought me awake:

There was a car parked out front.

Chapter 20

I'm not what the hyperventilating media would call a "gun nut," but right then I wished I owned a firearm.

I turned from the window and started to punch 911. I didn't think it was a good idea to call Detective Bean at this hour. I wanted to retain her goodwill. I had my finger on the last "1" when I heard a door slam.

Someone wanting to do me harm probably would shut the door softly. For that matter, they probably would not pull up in front of the house. I canceled the call and decided to wait. It was only about five seconds but it felt a lot longer. Even though I was expecting someone, I gasped and started when the bell rang.

I had to clear my throat in order to speak; my heart was hitting *that* hard and high in my chest.

"Who's there?" I yelled.

"It's Raylene," said the voice.

My world changed there and then. Fear gave way to relief and an overriding sadness was replaced with hope. I knew she had signed with that dirtbag attorney Dickson, but even if she was here to explain why, I wanted to see a familiar, maybe-friendly face. I went to the door, unlocked it, saw my senior waitperson standing there—in civvies—and smiled at her. Her expression was blank when I opened the door; it twisted into something resembling a smile as she gave a little "hi" motion with her hand and walked in.

"It's really good to see you," I told her. Then I asked, suddenly concerned, "Is there news?"

"No," she said. "Nothing new with A.J. and Thom. Which is a good thing, I guess."

I nodded and shut the door. She took a few small steps in. We stood facing one another, she in the center of the room, me with my back to the door. The cats emerged from wherever they had been hiding to wind round and round her legs. She bent to pet them.

"How are you?" I asked, just to break the strained silence.

"Been better," she replied.

"I guess all of us have been," I said. "Do you want anything? Tea? Beer?"

"No thanks. Just stopped and had a boilermaker on the way over. That's enough."

"You had to tank up to face me?" I asked. There was no sense pussyfooting, even with pussies at her feet.

"I had to do it to face myself," she answered. "That's why I sat out there at the top of the street, just working up the courage to come here."

"Why?" I asked.

"To tell you that I can't do it."

"Can't do what?"

"The lawsuit. You do know about that, right?" she asked.

I nodded.

"Well, I can't be part of it," she said. "I can't. I was thinking about it all day, ashamed that I had even agreed to let that man represent me. Not even me," she laughed mirthlessly. "He said he was representing 'my interests,' whatever those are."

"Collecting vintage Barbie dolls," I teased.

"Yeah, that's not what he was doing . . . though with the money he thought we'd get, I probably could've bought a really, really mint Barbie Penthouse on eBay," she smiled. The smile faded quickly. "I know the legal stuff isn't against you, really. And I know that whatever money we might get wouldn't come from your bank account, either. But it's wrong."

"You don't know what it means to hear you say that."

"I sorta do," she said. "It means that if I can get the others to see it that way, we can work on rebuilding the deli instead of building walls between us."

"True, but it means a lot more than that," I said. "You know there was nothing I, we, *anyone* could have done to foresee this, to prevent it. We still don't even know who did it and why. How do you intercept something like that?"

"I don't know," she said. "All I know is that I

know this would've broke your uncle's heart and I know it's probably doing the same to you. I had to come here before I went to see the others. I didn't want you to spend the night thinking about it, because I know that's exactly what you would've done."

"True enough," I admitted. "Can I ask what got you to that point?"

"Spending the money in my head," she said. "I asked myself if that's who I really am. I mean, if money was so important, I could sell this gorgeous body of mine, right?"

"To a certain clientele," I suggested.

"The kind who appreciate a vintage wine," she laughed. "I hear ya. Thing is, I'm not about money. I have enough to do everything I want to do. I love our little coop, I love our farmer, and I love our mama hen—Thom, I mean. And Thom? She'd never go along with this. That would set us against you *and* against her. We'd never recover from that. And for what? Stuff to put on my shelf?"

I went over and embraced her. She hugged me back. We stood there for a minute or more. I felt her warm tears on my neck and I held her tighter.

"I have to confess something," I said into her ear.

"I hope it's not something that's gonna make me feel like I just did something very stupid," she said.

"No," I assured her. "Until you did this, I wasn't

even sure I wanted to rebuild. Now, nothing's going to stop me."

We gripped each other tighter and I sniffed back my own little wave of emotion. The cats mewed—with jealousy or with approval, I did not know. Or care. This was one of those moments that, whenever the night was cold or the horizon was bleak, would warm me to the soles of my feet.

I whispered my thanks and then, without another word, with just a tight grin to hold back tears and relief in her eyes, she turned and left.

I sat for a while on the sofa, thinking about the courage Raylene had shown, when I suddenly remembered what I'd promised her. That the deli would return.

"Okay," I said to myself. "You've made that commitment. Now what?"

The strange thing was—and this was something I had done for my entire life—I didn't hit a pause button and reconsider. I didn't ask myself, "*Pitzel*, is that really what *you* want?" I had made a promise to someone I'd known not even two years and now I intended to honor that promise.

Is this the way it's supposed to work? I wondered. Life. *My* life. Shouldn't I decide what's best for me and then let everyone else try and fit their lives into that? That was what most people did. *But Raylene hadn't done that,* I told myself. She had just taken the tougher, less convenient road, turning down easy money for the chance to go back to work.

The phone rang. The landline. Only my staff had that. I grabbed the call in the kitchen.

It was Newt.

"Please don't hang up," he said. "Please."

"I won't," I assured him.

"Boss, I messed up, I know it. And I'm not asking you to give me a pass on that. Oh, and I am sorry I'm calling so late. But I wanted you to know that I got a text from Raylene saying she just was talking to you about the lawsuit and I'm totally onboard with her. That dude Dickson—I told him what I did with Benjamin and he told me that had nothing to do with this thing. He said I could still get money. I know you're not going to believe this, but money had nothing to do with me helping him. I—Jesus, I just didn't want to be a short-order cook anymore. He had a way out. And I honestly don't know if I want to be a cook when you reopen, which Raylene said you want to do. All I know is I don't want you to hate me. Going with Dickson—"

He ended abruptly. I thought he was going to say more and I hadn't formulated a response.

"Boss?"

"I'm here," I said. My voice was flat. No, more than that. It was unforgiving.

This was not a teenager I was talking to. It was a man. A young man, a provincial man, but a man. A man who had made a dumb decision and abetted industrial espionage. Now he was looking for absolution. I didn't know if he had actually snubbed Dickson or if, based on my response, he'd go back to him. I hated the fact that I trusted Newt so little because of what he'd done.

But what if it *had* been a stupid, spur-of-the-moment mistake?

Didn't I come down here on an impulse? I asked myself. *Didn't I run from my former husband, from my career, from my hometown—all because I needed a life preserver, any life preserver?*

And I had a decade on Newt. The guy could be truly repentant. And while I had a right to be angry, was it smart to *stay* angry? What I said and did now was going to ripple through both our lives.

"Please say something," he said. "Even if it's to tell me—"

"Welcome back," I said.

I heard a small intake of air, like someone sucking a hit of helium from a balloon. Which was an appropriate metaphor, since Newt's voice was higher when he swore from relief and thanked me.

"Don't thank me," I said. "Just learn this much: when you have a problem, take it to your friends. Take it to the people who care about you, not people who want to use you."

"I'm shaking," he said. "I've never felt like this."

"Like how?"

"So scared," he said. "Somebody tried to sell me a swamp and I came really close to trying to build a future on it. My granpaw did that in

Louisiana but there was a market for alligator skins then."

It wasn't an entirely successful analogy, but I wasn't going to dispute it then and there. Especially because my cell phone was ringing.

"How about I call you in a day or two and we all get together?" I said. "I've got someone on the cell."

"It's a deal," he said. "And thank you. Thank you."

"Thank *you*," I said—not as enthusiastically as him, but enough to leave the door open to continue repairing the relationship.

I took the incoming call. I had thought it might be A.J. Two or Luke or Dani also backing out of the suit. It was none of the above. It was Detective Bean.

"I know it's very late, Gwen, but I'm still at work. You got a second?" she asked.

I wanted to comment that this was ironic, given that just before I had been concerned about calling *her* too late. But I held that thought.

"Of course." I heard something new in her voice. It was not a question but a demand, the vocal equivalent of a bloodhound suddenly tugging back on the leash.

"There was a big plastic trash can in the kitchen," she said. "Where was it?"

"We keep—kept—that next to the food prep table," I told her. "All the food discards go in there. You know, when you slam down the head of lettuce and pull out the heart? That goes in. Cucumber peels. Carrot scrapings. Potato skins."

"Any caffeinated beverages?"

"Never," I said. "I don't—didn't—allow coffee or soda in the prep area. Why?"

"I'd rather not get into that just now," she said.

"Why?" I pressed. I hadn't said "why" twice like that since I was ten or so.

"You know the answer to that," she said. "This is a police matter—"

"About *my* deli!"

"—and we want to look into this on our own."

"Detective, I have a reputation for quality deli. You may not know this, but I apply that standard to every facet of my life."

"That's not what they call it here," she said.

No, I had to admit. They called it meddling. I hated the word, especially since I wasn't limited by due process and I got results.

"All right," I said, affecting acquiescence. "But for my peace of mind, can you at least tell me if you think this was directed at me or at the politicians."

"I cannot give out that information."

"Because you don't have it?"

"Because I don't want anything interfering with our investigation, which I must get back to now," the detective said. "Thank you for your help."

"But I may have information that—"

"If I need anything else, I'll call," she said curtly. "I promise."

The detective hung up. I stood by the end table brooding. I almost missed Grant, who, for all his flaws, often whispered sweet privileged

information in my ear. But I quickly got a grip.
Still, for all the joy and *nachas* I felt at the partial
return of my beloved coworkers—my family—
the truth was I had no idea who had attacked
my real home or why. That not only rankled,
it frightened me. Paranoia about hate crimes is
only paranoia when there's no foundation for
one's fears.

I paced the living room until I realized I was
hungry, then went and had some gherkins and
put the coffeepot on. The cats wandered in as
they invariably did when I went into the kitchen.
I saw that their bowls still had the dregs of
kibble.

"Finish what's there," I commanded. "Kittens
are starving in Brooklyn alleyways."

I considered the situation and what little information I had, as the cats rubbed my legs.

"I survived the explosion," I said. "If someone
were after me, they would still be after me. I
would have heard from them, gotten some kind
of warning, like whitefish wrapped with a warning that I'd end up in the lake."

That hadn't happened and my gut told me I
wasn't the target. I went to the computer and
checked the schedules of the mayoral candidates. None of the three had altered their
schedules. There was an item about amped-up
security, but that was to be expected after a
bombing regardless of the target. There were
no news items about threats to any of the cam-
paigns.

"What about Benjamin and Grace?" I asked

myself. Would they have blown my place up so they could swoop in and buy the site for a proverbial song—specifically, something from the old Barbra Streisand show *I Can Get It for You Wholesale?*

That was possible . . . except for the fact that Benjamin had been in the basement.

"Unless your gal-pal wanted you dead," I thought aloud. Except that she was in the dining area and could just as easily have been hurt or killed if the floor gave way. She would have had no way of knowing exactly what would happen.

Which left me with bupkes.

I sat at the kitchen table with my special McNulty's coffee. In the handful of puzzles that had come my way, none had ever been so empty of clues.

I sipped.

"That's not true," I mumbled. Detective Bean knew something that she wasn't sharing. From the sound of it, there was a remnant of a coffee or tea container in the debris. It couldn't belong to my staff since we ate and drank in the dining section. My homeless Dumpster visitor didn't come around with a beverage. And—I thought back—Sandy kept a thermos in the cab of her van. I remembered because we usually filled it.

Unless—

I sat up.

Unless that wasn't what Detective Bean meant.

I thought back. I sipped. I slumped toward my coffee mug and thought some more. I sipped.

And then something suddenly didn't fit. I sat upright.

"Is it possible?" I asked myself.

My brain was racing. Something didn't fit, then two things didn't fit, then suddenly a bunch of things *did* fit.

If I was right, I was going to need some help.

I made a call. Then I made another. Then I got a good night's sleep before I made just one more.

Chapter 21

"Boy, am I glad to hear from you!"

Kane Iger sounded genuinely thrilled when he picked up the phone.

"You're sure it's not too early?" I asked apologetically.

"It's never too early to seek the aid of Captain Health," he said. He laughed. "Sorry. I couldn't resist. It really is good hear from you, Gwen. How are you?"

"Eh," I answered. "Listen, strange as it may seem, I sort of do need the assistance of Captain Health," I told him.

"Really?"

"Yes, really." I could practically see the child-like smile on his big, open face. "I have a feeling I know who attacked my deli and I want to do some checking—but I don't want to do it alone."

"You've come to the right man," he said. "Who and where?"

"Would you mind coming here before work? I

have some things I want to pull together. Then we can go together."

"It's a deal," he said. "Gee, I'm so glad you're not angry at me."

"I didn't say that, Kane. Benjamin is a skunk, but what you wanted to do was pretty wrong."

"Like you said, the man is no good," Kane said. "One way or another, I wanted to see justice done."

"We can discuss your tactics later," I told him. "Right now, I need someone strong to give me a hand. Just promise you won't go off half-cocked."

"You have the word of Kane Iger and Captain Health," he said.

I gave him my address and he said he'd be there in a half hour.

"See you then," I told him.

I went to my laptop and pulled up all the information I could find on the life and times of Josephine Young, all the articles on her restaurant, and printed them out. I got a yellow marker and started highlighting specific sections, making notes. I spread them on the coffee table, stacked some of them on the floor, then grabbed a few online ads from Gar McQueen. I read those over, added a few yellow lines, put them in a separate pile.

Exactly thirty minutes later, the doorbell rang. I raised the shade of the window beside it, looked out, saw Kane Iger standing there. He waved at me through the window.

"A woman can never be too cautious," he said as I opened the door.

He stood on the threshold a moment, towering over me like the statue of Atlas at Rockefeller Center. He looked at me with a sweet, satisfied little smile.

"What is it?" I asked.

"Just happy," he said. "Happy you asked me over."

"So—you gonna come in?"

The big man entered, hands cupped in front of himself, waiting for directions. I gestured toward the sofa.

"Wow. Someone's been doing some homework."

"Yeah," I said. "I am even more determined to find the putz who put a hole in my floor."

"You seem to have some ideas," he said.

"One," I told him.

He eased his large frame around the coffee table. "The dancer," he said. "What makes you think it was her . . . or," he added as he saw the second pile, "the landscaper? Or both?"

"Hey, before we get into all that, you want anything?"

"What've you got?"

"The usual beverages plus decaf in a can, though I can't imagine you'd be able to endure that."

"I'll take a club soda if you have one," he said.

I left to get a Canada Dry. "You didn't bring your thermos?" I called from the kitchen.

"Only when I've made it fresh, and there wasn't time," he said.

I poured and went back to the living room. "It's probably kinda flat, but them's the breaks."

"That would make it just plain water, which is fine," he said charitably.

I handed it to him and looked down at the documents I'd printed out. "Hey, I hear you met a friend of mine at the hospital the other day."

"Oh? Who?"

"Bonnie Potts."

"Poor kid with the compound fracture? Yes . . . what a sweetheart. She really took a hit. How do you know her?"

"Her grandfather is my butcher," I said.

"I see. So, are you going to show me what you have?"

"Well, it's sort of along the lines of what you had on Benjamin and Grace," I said. "Just a big, fat hunch."

"Hunches are usually good starting points," he said.

I gestured toward the sofa and he flopped down. I remained standing, my arms folded as I glanced at this man who helped kids through some of the worst times of their lives. "I have a question, first."

"Okay. Shoot."

"How did you know how I take my coffee?"

He seemed surprised by the question. "What do you mean? I didn't know."

"The other day in the van. You poured almond milk for yourself but gave me mine black, no sugar. Most of the people I know at least take some kind of sweetener."

"Huh. I guess I figured you'd ask for it if you wanted it."

"Is that what it was?" I inquired.

"Sure. What else?"

"I was sitting here thinking that maybe you knew how I took it."

"How would I know that? *Why* would I know that?"

"Damn good question, Kane. How and why. Did you maybe come to the deli and see me pour one of my bottomless cups of coffee as I worked the counter or went back and forth to my office?"

"I've been to your deli once," he said. There was a little squeak in his voice, the kind you hear when someone is trying to get through a lie.

"When was that?"

"I don't know. A couple of months ago. Say, what is this? An interrogation? Are you going to read me my Miranda rights next?"

"Maybe someone should," I said. "What this is, Kane, is me wanting to know if you cased my place before you went to Alex Storm's butcher shop," I said. "I called Bonnie's mother. You went there to drop off a signed photo for her. A photo she hadn't asked for. Oh, and my guess is also to put a homemade bomb in a container of chopped liver."

Kane rose. "You're crazy."

"Am I?" I backed away. "You went to the shop, not Bonnie's home, not to the hospital. You went when there were two days of protests going on and Alex was distracted."

"You think that's my fault too?"

"Not *too*," I said. "It was just convenient, one of the reasons you selected me as a target."

"Why would I do that? I *help* people, remember?"

"I do, which is why I kept wondering why you were not only willing to frame Benjamin and Grace, you were eager to do so. Why?"

"Because they're stinkers," he said without hesitation.

"That's true, but they're not the stinkers who blew up my deli. You did." I looked into those innocent eyes, which suddenly seemed more belligerent than heroic. "You used the fertilizer from your little organic farm to do that, didn't you?"

"That is the dumbest thing you've said yet, and you've said some pretty stupid things."

"Uh-uh. Here's my theory, Kane, the unified theory of Kane Iger. You take this hero thing seriously, which is all well and good when you're dealing with kids. But I'm thinking you want to be a hero so bad you're willing to commit crimes in order to solve them—blaming someone else, of course."

"You're ridiculous. And you're a liar." He swatted the papers on the coffee table. "You never suspected the dancer. These are props."

"Good deduction, Captain."

"You did this to entrap me."

"Don't try and put this on me, Kane. You

planned the whole thing pretty carefully. Hell, you probably knew I was going to be at the hospital to see my workers and hung out till I showed up. Or maybe you watched me when you got off work, followed me there. You wanted to know who I suspected, who the police suspected, so you could finish the job by planting evidence. Evidence which would have been really credible since it was the exact same stuff you used to make your damn bomb!"

I saw a struggle going on in his brain, the battle between wanting to do right and wanting to choke the life from me.

"You have no proof," he said, finally moving from around the coffee table, "just your own stupid theories. *I* have a theory. You blew up your own deli to collect the insurance. You were willing to sacrifice your own workers, your own customers, just to make money. I see it all the time in the bank, greedy people, hungry people, wanting to destroy in order to make their own lives more comfortable. You're no different from them."

"That's not going to stick," I said.

"Yes it will," Kane said. "They'll find you here with bomb-making material. You were jealous of Josephine Young. Even our moron local police will see that. You were tired of competing, you just wanted out."

"That isn't going to work, Kane," I said.

"Oh? Why not?"

"Because there was coffee bean residue in the

bomb debris," I told him. "As we speak, those 'moron local police' are analyzing something I pulled from my hamper."

"Gwen's dirty laundry," he said. "How fitting. What are they analyzing?"

"Jeans I spilled some of your coffee on."

Kane stopped, rigid, as if he'd been hit by a freeze ray. His expression seemed suddenly far off. Someone was threatening his Bat Cave. He looked like he wanted to rush there *now*. His eyes roamed the nonexistent horizon for a moment before settling back on me.

"You," he said accusingly. "You are *evil*. From the moment we met, you were jealous because of how I helped children. Children are your kryptonite because you don't have any. They are the reason you're bad."

Turning things I'd said against me, that was both low and clever. I didn't bother to answer.

"I'm going to solve a crime," he said, backing me toward the front door. "*This* crime. The crime of who beat your brains out."

I tried to slip off to the side, toward the kitchen. He adjusted his approach. I was scared. My legs were liquefying. I often wondered how people got backed into corners. Now I knew: they did it to themselves from fear.

"It was Gar McQueen," Kane went on. "He was working on behalf of Josephine Young. You suspected this might happen and they knew it. I'll testify to that."

"Don't do this," I said. "Think of all the kids you're going to disappoint."

"You're going to rat me out anyway, Katz-woman, Mistress of the Wicked. I have to silence you."

"You don't," I pleaded. "You're only making it worse."

He laughed. He probably didn't realize it, but it was a good villainous mwah-ha-ha. "How can *I* make things worse?"

"You can take a bullet in the backside," a voice said from the kitchen.

Kane spun as Detective Bean walked into the living room, steady and resolute behind her firearm. One of the calls I'd made was to Bonnie Potts; one of the calls I'd made was to Kane; and one of the calls I'd made was to the police. She'd parked around the corner on Adamwood Drive, with backup, and arrived a few minutes before Kane did.

The big man froze.

"Put your hands on top of your head," Bean said.

Two other officers emerged behind her. One was holding a Taser, the other had plastic hand restraints.

Kane hesitated. I could see it in his flaring nostrils and rapid breathing, he was thinking of going down fighting, like Captain Health would want.

"You don't need to die," I said softly to him. "You need to get help."

"Captain Health *gives* help, he doesn't accept it."

"Hey, even those little kids in the hospital know when they need some care," I reminded him. "Surely Captain Health is as smart as they are."

His expression changed faster than a speeding bullet. Tears piled up in his eyes.

"Captain Health is invulnerable," he said, his lower lip shaking.

"You're not in costume," I said. "We got you in your civilian identity."

He remained where he was and began to sob. "That wasn't fair."

"Maybe not," I said. "I guess you'll just have to wait for the sequel to make things right."

He submitted quietly, peaceably to the restraints. One of the officers radioed for backup to swing around the block. Within moments, sirens cracked the early morning. They escorted him out while Bean holstered her weapon.

"Nicely done," she said to me. "Very nicely done."

"How much of it will be admissible in court?" I asked.

"None of this, except the charges you're going to file for attempted assault," she said. "But the jeans and your testimony will give us enough to get a search warrant. His garden will do the rest."

I looked out the open door at unfamiliar faces appearing in windows I rarely looked at. I suddenly missed New York, where I knew everyone on the floor of my apartment building.

Bean made sure I was okay before following her team back to book the Bank Bomber—as

I was sure Candy Sommerton and her colleagues would dub him. I felt profound sadness as they pulled away. I'd not only helped to bring down a hero to some local kids, I'd lost a guy who was a pretty attentive date.

But then I smiled. The smile became a chuckle and then the chuckle became a laugh.

Only in the world of Gwen Katz could a case involving coffee be cracked by Detective Bean.

Chapter 22

We gathered in the hospital room, displeasing the floor nurses and doctors. But they looked the other way because, unorthodox as it was, the big group hug was turning out to be just what the patient needed.

Luke and Dani, Raylene and A.J. Two, and I all met in A.J.'s room at noon. My waitperson had woken up during the night and one of the first things she asked for, after water and a bedpan, was that her closest friends come by to give her some good, loving energy. She mentioned all of us by name. She was going to be okay.

"I gotta be," she wheezed when we'd begun to gather. "While I was knocked out . . . I realized I didn't like . . . Louis Dunn . . . or Tootsie Pearl. I'm gonna vote . . . for Moss Post."

"Me too," I told her.

Thom was wheeled in after we arrived, pushed by Newt. If crying was good energy, then we had it to spare; the gathering was as healing for us as it was for the patient. About the only thing missing was Tiny Tim wandering in, propped on a little crutch, saying, "God bless us, every one!"

Thinking of Tiny Tim made me think of Kane Iger. Detective Bean told me that the analysis of my jeans matched the coffee bean traces from the explosion; there would be long weeks of psych evaluation before the district attorney decided what to do with the man.

It was all depressing and tragic, especially the call from Benjamin and Grace early that morning. They'd seen Candy's report on, yes, the Bank Bomber and my role in nabbing him. Benjamin apologized again for everything that had happened and I forgave him—especially after he said they'd decided not to open a deli after all and canceled the property purchase he was going to make here for that purpose.

I was happy to see them go.

Thom walked us through a little prayer and, though I'm usually more than a little cynical about that sort of thing, I went along. It actually felt good. Not because of the prayer per se, but because of what I said at the top of my little narrative.

These were the people I needed and who needed me.

This was family.